MW01041799

The
PERILOUS YEAR

The

PERILOUS YEAR

CONNIE BRUMMEL CROOK

Fitzhenry & Whiteside

Fitzhenry & Whiteside, 195 Allstate Parkway, Markham, Ontario L3R 4T8
In the United States, 121 Harvard Avenue, Suite 2, Allston, Massachusetts 02134

www.fitzhenry.ca   godwit@fitzhenry.ca

10 9 8 7 6 5 4 3 2 1

National Library of Canada Cataloguing in Publication
Crook, Connie Brummel
The perilous year / Connie Brummel Crook.

ISBN 1-55041-816-5 (bound).–ISBN 1-55041-818-1 (pbk.)

I. Title.
PS8555.R6113P47 2003   jC813'.54   C2003-900595-X
PZ7.C8818Pe 2003

U.S. Publisher Cataloging-in-Publication Data
(Library Congress Standards)
Crook, Connie Brummel.
The perilous year / Connie Brummel Crook.—1st ed.
[144] p. : cm.
Summary: A family's rural experience of the late 1700's. Father brings a stepmother
home for his twin boys, and so begins a difficult period of adjustment.
Sequel to: The hungry year.

ISBN 1-55041-816-5
ISBN 1-55041-818-1 (pbk.)
1. Canada – History – 1791-1841 – Juvenile fiction. 2. Stepmothers – Fiction – Juvenile lit-
erature. (1. Canada – History – 1791-1841 – Fiction. 2. Stepmothers – Fiction.) I. Title.
[Fic] 21   PZ7.C881Pe 2003

Fitzhenry & Whiteside acknowledges with thanks the Canada Council for the Arts,
the Government of Canada through the Book Publishing Industry Development Program
(BPIDP), the Ontario Arts Council and the Government of Ontario through the Ontario
Media Development Corporation's Ontario Book Initiative for their support for
our publishing program.

Design and Layout: Tanya Montini for TM+CO.
Cover image: David Craig
Printed and bound in Canada

To my grandsons,
Alex and Ryan Floyd
and
their younger brother, Jordan Floyd,
who wants the next book to be Geordie's story:
with love, and thanks for answering many questions.

CONTENTS

ACKNOWLEDGEMENTS

I thank the many Ontario students that took part in the 2002 Silver Birch reading program who requested a sequel to *The Hungry Year* and gave helpful suggestions. I especially thank Lee Johnston of Kingsway Park Public School in Thunder Bay, who asked if I would write a sequel about the twins when they were older. This request triggered my thoughts to this story.

Once again, thanks to Katherine A. Staples, former manager of the Loyalist Cultural Centre at Adolphustown, Ontario, for sending me files and maps preserved from the times of early settlements in Adolphustown and Fredericksburgh townships and for answering so cheerfully my many questions about that time period in Canadian history. Thanks also to Pam Dickey of Buckhorn, Ontario for advice about clothing, and Rob Bruce of Belleville for facts about bears.

Thanks to my cousins Thornton and Doris Brummel of Napanee, Ontario, for their research and answers to questions about the Napanee and Hay Bay areas where they have lived most of their lives. Also, thanks to my cousins Diana Maxwell and Gerald McKeown of Prince Edward County, Ontario, for answering questions about the geography, history, and waters of the area where they live.

A special thanks to Dorothy Rowan Floyd, who told me about her experiences with two of her babies. The method she followed to correct club feet (Mary Ann's ailment) without surgery could well have been followed by devoted mothers in times past.

A very special thanks to Fitzhenry & Whiteside: to Laura Peetoom for helpful suggestions and editing, and to Gail Winskill and Sharon Fitzhenry for encouragement.

Connie Brummel Crook

PART ONE

Kate and the Twins

CHAPTER
ONE

"Quiet!" whispered Alex. "I hear someone coming!" The eleven-year-old boy and his twin brother, Ryan, were crouched behind a tangle of chokecherry vines at the edge of the Shaws' bush. The late-April sun was low in the sky, sending shadows in among the cedar and spruce trees.

Ryan stood up and looked through a gap in the branches. "Looks like two people sitting on stumps by the stable," he said.

"Two people? Let me see!"

Alex brushed his straight blond hair off his forehead and looked through the branches.

"Hey! It's Albert Shaw! And Kate's beside him."

The two boys gave each other knowing looks.

"Didn't I tell you, Ryan?" said Alex. "It's no wonder Albert's gotten so boring. He never takes us fishing anymore and he isn't even funny the way he used to be!"

"I guess that's what love does to you!" said the thoughtful Ryan.

"Yuck! If that's what it does, I'm never going to be in love!" said Alex.

"Will you stop yelling! They'll find out we're here ... now listen!"

Kate's voice was clearer now. "I just don't know, Bertie," she was saying. "I'm seventeen, but Father still needs me. And so do my brothers."

"Bertie!" Alex choked. "She's calling him Bertie!"

"Yes, but did you hear what else Kate said? She said, 'Father needs me.'" Ryan wondered out loud, "You don't think Albert wants to take Kate away? You don't suppose he really wants to ... "

"... marry her!" Alex finished Ryan's sentence. Then they looked at each other, speechless.

After a while, Alex said reassuringly, "Albert is twenty. He's much too old to marry our sister. And besides, he hasn't even asked Father's permission to court our Kate."

Ryan nodded. "I'll be glad when Father gets back from King's Town. He'll put an end to that."

"Well, Father isn't here. So who's going to stop this?"

Ryan peeked out over Alex's shoulder. He couldn't believe his eyes. Albert Shaw was holding both of his sister's hands, and she was looking up at him.

Forgetting to be quiet, Alex pushed a branch out of the way, to get a better view.

"Shhh!" hissed Ryan, but his warning wasn't necessary. They could have trampled the bush like bears, and Kate and Albert would not have noticed. The twins stared helplessly as Albert put his left arm around Kate's waist. They gasped in shock as Albert bent over and kissed Kate on the forehead.

Sarah Shaw's brother was kissing their Kate!

That did it! At the very same moment, Ryan and Alex charged out from the shelter of the trees. "Stop! Stop!" they yelled in unison.

"What … what are you two doing out here?" gasped Kate, still holding Albert's hand. "I thought you were playing checkers inside with Nancy and Betsy."

"We thought you went to the barn dance with Sarah," said Ryan. "And we thought Albert was going to go fishing with us."

"But he said he was too busy — and now we know why," said Alex. The two boys glared at their sister.

"It's time you two were in bed," said Kate.

"No!" said Ryan and Alex, still glaring.

"March over there, right now!" She pointed to a small log cabin not far from the Shaws' house. It was the first shanty they built when they'd arrived in Fredericksburgh Township on the shores of Lake Ontario in 1784. Candlelight flickered from the shanty's tiny window.

Kate was sharing Sarah's bedroom in the main house, a five-room cabin with a loft. But even the larger house could become too crowded — with Mr. and Mrs. Shaw, five children, Grandma Shaw, and guests. So the boys had been sleeping in the old building. It was fun to have a place to themselves, but Alex kept up the delaying tactics. "Where's Sarah?" he asked. "Why didn't you go to the barn dance with her?"

"Alex Shaw, what I do is my own business!" Kate's words were tart, but her brown eyes looked kind as she stared down at her brothers. She wasn't angry anymore. The moon had just appeared, and it was making her auburn hair sparkle. Albert had been standing there the whole time, gazing at her. Ryan thought he looked foolish.

"Listen," Kate said, the corners of her mouth twitching into a smile, "you two don't need to look out for me! I'm just fine. Bertie and I are going to the barn dance in a while. We were just having a little talk first."

There was that horrible name — Bertie!

Alex glared at Albert, who pretended not to notice. "Talk?" Alex growled. "You were *kissing*! We saw you!"

Albert frowned. "Your father is coming home soon, boys, and he'll settle you two for spying on your sister."

"You think so?" said Alex. "Father hardly ever scolds us! And we'll tell him everything, Kate."

"Yeah!" said Ryan.

"Fine," said Kate. "You do that. But first you'll go to bed. Albert, will you excuse me? I think I'd better tuck these two in."

Alex and Ryan grabbed Kate's hands, and Albert turned swiftly and headed back to the house.

"I'll be over shortly, Bertie. I promise," Kate called out. Then she marched the twins over to the shanty.

Alex raised his eyebrows at his brother and winked.

Ryan gave his brother a knowing smile. The twins were quite different, but they understood each other well.

CHAPTER
TWO

"Whatever happened, Kate?" asked Sarah. "James and I kept watching for you all evening."

Rays of yellow sunlight streamed through the three east windows of the Shaws' kitchen and right across the long maple table and side benches. The whole Shaw family and three O'Carrs were sitting there, eating breakfast. Alex was on Kate's left and Ryan on her right. The two boys looked smugly at each other and then grinned at Albert, sitting on the other side, staring silently at his plate. He didn't notice.

Kate was also eating in silence and not even looking up. Sarah shook her head at her brother and her best friend. "Say ... did you two have a fight?" she asked, and Albert and Kate both flushed red.

"Oh, dear! I'm always putting my foot in my mouth. I'm sorry." Sarah smoothed back a few strands of bright red hair that had fallen out from under her mob cap. Her grey-green eyes studied her brother and then her friend.

"Don't worry, Sarah," said Kate. "Everything's all right. Alex had a stomach ache, and I couldn't leave him.

I made up the extra bed in the old cabin and slept there all night."

"Oh, I see," said Sarah. She looked at Alex, wolfing down a thick slice of bread covered with globs of butter and strawberry jam, and narrowed her eyes. "He seems fine this morning."

"Sarah, let the boys enjoy their breakfast," said Mrs. Shaw, adjusting her cap, which had slipped to the side of her head as she was stirring the oatmeal porridge. "Albert and Kate aren't complaining about missing the dance. So why should you?"

"Because it isn't fair that Kate always has to … "

"Sarah, that's enough," said the big, red-headed Mr. Shaw in a low, but firm voice. He was buttering a thick slice of bread at the other end of the table. Sarah shut her lips together tightly.

Grandma Shaw looked at her son and then turned to Kate. "If one of the boys has another attack tonight, just call me, Kate. I'll watch over them. There'll be no shenanigans, I can tell you. It's too bad you and Bertie couldn't have gone to the barn dance together. You need to get out with other young people instead of staying in and working all the time." She shook her head and stared right back at Mr. Shaw, who was frowning.

"It's all right," said Kate, smiling at Grandma Shaw. She'd loved Grandma Shaw like her own grandma ever since she had met her six years before. That was the year Father had brought her and the boys to their new land. They were like orphans at the time because their own mother and grandmother had died. They had taken instantly to Grandma Shaw.

"Things will be changing, Kate," Grandma Shaw was saying. "Mark my words. You'll see!" Grandma Shaw gave Kate a warm smile.

"What'll she see?" asked Alex.

"Well, Ma. You've had your say," said Mr. Shaw, still chewing on his slice of bread. "But don't be telling secrets that aren't yours to give away."

"You're right, Will," said Grandma Shaw. "I won't add another word. Except, of course, to say that you'll be finding out soon enough."

"Finding out what?" Alex and Ryan screeched in unison.

Mr. Shaw cleared his throat and stared at the boys. "After breakfast, you two are going down to the barn to help with the chores. Your father said that I was to put you to work till he got back. Albert will tell you what to do."

Ryan looked at his brother. Alex shrugged. "Father should have been back by now. What's taking him so long?" he asked, trying another tack. "It's been three weeks!"

"Not one to leave mysteries alone, are you, young man!" said Mr. Shaw, raising a bushy eyebrow.

"The boy's right — it has been a long time," said Grandma Shaw. "And with the spring farm work and all, it's high time Mr. O'Carr came home to his family."

"You don't suppose Father was caught by pirates, do you?" said Kate, looking worried.

"Pirates!" exclaimed Mrs. Shaw as she ladled out bacon and eggs from the iron-spider frying pan. "On Lake Ontario?"

"It's been known," said Mr. Shaw. "But they never bother us settlers — except for a meal or two. They look for bigger prey. Though lately I've heard tell—" At Mrs. Shaw's frown, he stopped, much to the boys' disappointment. "There's never been a pirate in Hay Bay, anyway," Mr. Shaw assured Kate.

"Well, robbers, then," said Kate. "Maybe someone found out he was carrying all those pelts he trapped over the winter. Maybe they robbed him and beat him up!"

"You're all such worriers!" said Mrs. Shaw. "If he's delayed, it's because he had other business to do in King's Town that he didn't tell you anything about. Now eat your eggs, everybody, before they get cold!"

Silence fell as the two families set to the serious work of finishing their breakfasts.

"Hoo-hu-woo!"

"Is that you, Alex?" Ryan whispered from behind the barn. He was trying to get Bobcat to come down from the ash tree where he was hiding. Then he remembered. "Hoo-hu-woo!" he called back.

Alex bounded around the corner and scrambled up to Bobcat's perch. "Good old owl call worked again!" said Alex, grinning down at his brother.

"Yep, it sure is handy!"

The black-striped cat swished his short tail, but he allowed Alex to carry him down.

"Good old Bobcat," said Ryan fondly, stroking the cat's coarse fur. "What have you been up to all day?"

Bobcat came and went as he pleased, and sometimes

they didn't see him for days. But he was important to the O'Carr family. Long ago, he'd kept the twins and their sister alive, bringing them rabbits and other animals he hunted during the savage winter of the Hungry Year when the twins were small. He had played with them and kept them happy when Father, out hunting, was wounded and didn't come back for many days.

"I know what I've been up to," complained Alex. "Shovelling manure … that's got to be the longest day on a farm ever!"

"Right … and then for a treat we get to go out and spread it out on the field. What a life, being a farmer!"

"I'd rather be a hunter, like Bobcat. Forget all this ploughing and milking stuff!"

"Or like Tówi," Ryan said wistfully. "It's too bad Father didn't marry Gajijáwa. Then Tówi would have been our brother, and we could have hunted with him all day long!"

"Yeah, that would have been all right."

The two boys were quiet, remembering how much the two Mohawks had helped them during the Hungry Year.

"Well, it's too late now," said Alex. "Gajijáwa married someone else. Now, let's go in and see what's for supper. I'm starving!"

"I think Mrs. Shaw said she was cooking an old hen."

"Yuck … oh, well, better than nothing. And maybe she made dumplings!"

There *were* dumplings, and they were about to be served supper when Alex and Ryan heard Father's horses and wagon pulling into the laneway. The twins stood not far from the Shaws' front door and waited.

"What do you suppose he brought us this time?" asked Alex, his eyes shining eagerly.

"I don't really care," said Ryan. "I just want Father back."

"Me, too," said Alex. "I'm sick of working for Albert and Mr. Shaw. We're visitors and should be treated like visitors."

"Well, we've been here a long time. You know what Kate says."

"What?"

"Visitors are like fish — after three days, they start to smell," said Ryan. "I'd rather be like a horse, and pull my weight."

"Goody Two-Shoes," grumbled Alex. And then the wagon drew up beside them.

Father was sitting way up on the driver's seat, pulling back on the horses' reins to make them stop. His brown hair was trimmed like a city man's and he looked happier than he'd ever been, as far as the boys could remember. That was the first strange thing. The second strange thing made the boys forget to ask if Father had gotten an extra-good price for his pelts. They forgot everything. For right beside Father on the front seat sat — a woman!

She wasn't much older than Kate and her head was covered with a mass of thick, dark brown curls that fell to her forehead and framed the inner edges of her big straw hat. From it, two long red ostrich feathers protruded upright.

Father didn't seem to notice his boys' amazement. Smiling, he jumped down from the wagon, then turned his back to Alex and Ryan and held out his hand to the young woman. Her deep blue taffeta dress billowed out as she stepped onto the wagon's small iron side-step and hopped to the ground. Her hat had fallen forward a little and the feathers were bending over her face. She pushed the hat back before gazing solemnly at the boys.

"Boys," said Father, turning to his sons, who were looking at him now. "May I present the granddaughter of Lord and Lady Banks." The boys stared back at her in surprise. They had never met an aristocrat before. Her rosy cheeks and bright brown eyes looked friendly enough. But what was she doing out here with Father? Then Father added, "And she's your new *mother*."

Alex and Ryan gaped at the stranger in disbelief. It must be a joke. But why would Father make such a silly joke?

CHAPTER
THREE

"Cat got your tongue?" Father bellowed. "Where are your manners, boys?"

Alex and Ryan couldn't even answer. All they could do was stare at the woman with the red feathers.

"Well, never mind, David," said the woman. "It's been a long, rough journey from King's Town. I just want to go inside and freshen up." She brushed past the boys and headed for the house, her elegant dress swishing over the new spring grass. A young robin bounced along the ground, but the boys didn't notice it. They kept staring at the mass of blue taffeta moving toward the front door.

"Here, boys," said Father in a slightly gentler tone. "Take care of the horses." He handed the reins to Alex and brushed some road dust off his breeches.

"Are you really *married* to that lady?" asked Ryan, hoping it wasn't true.

"Yes, I am — and it's your job to make her feel welcome." Then he turned on his heel and walked briskly after his new wife.

Silently, the boys stabled the horses. The situation was

too unbelievable to talk about. Then they hurried back to the kitchen and the smell of bubbling chicken and fresh pot-pie dumplings simmering in a large iron pot over the fireplace.

Mrs. Redfeather was looking at Mrs. Shaw's fine English china. It had been shipped all the way from England and was brought out only for special occasions.

"I hope she breaks a plate," Alex whispered. "Then maybe Father will send her back to King's Town."

"She doesn't look like she's the type that breaks stuff," said Ryan.

"Well, Ann," said Mrs. Shaw, "we've heard so much about you. It's a delight to meet you in person."

"Heard so much *about* her!" Alex whispered angrily. "So did everybody know about her except us?"

"Yeah, and we're the ones that have to live with her for the rest of our lives."

"It's not fair."

Father turned and glared at the boys. He was one of those fathers who sees and hears everything. "What was that you said, Alex?"

"I said … it's not fair that we're the only ones who never heard about Ann."

"'Mother,' to you boys," Father blustered. "And you …"

Just then Kate and Sarah came bursting into the room, giggling and carrying handfuls of spotted yellow dog-tooth violets.

"Father! You're back!" Kate cried. "I was starting to worry. With all those fur pelts you were carrying, I was afraid someone had robbed you and left you by the side of the road!"

Father took his new wife by the arm.

"Ann," he said, "I want to introduce you to my daughter Kate."

Mrs. Redfeather stepped toward Father and smoothed out her dark blue dress.

"Kate, I want you to meet my wife and your new mother, Ann Stapley." Father coughed. "I mean Ann O'Carr. We were married two weeks ago in King's Town."

"Married?" Kate's voice trembled and the boys saw her hands shake. Sarah gasped and slipped her arm around Kate's shoulders. "Married? This is sudden, Father. You didn't say a word to me!"

"David!" said Father's new bride. "You mean you didn't tell … "

"Why should I tell the children? It would just have worried them. It's better this way."

"I don't see that this is better," said Ann. "What a shock!"

"So, Father … " Kate was swallowing hard. "Did you just meet her and decide to get married on the spot? Or … "

"No," Father said. "I met her father during the war. He's an army surgeon. You've heard me mention him and his wife, an aristocrat—the daughter of Lord and Lady Banks. You knew I visited the Stapleys in King's Town."

"But you never mentioned they had a daughter … just my age!"

"No," Father laughed, "but Ann's much older than you. She's twenty!"

"Twenty!" said Sarah. "That's only two-and-a-half years older than Kate!"

Mrs. Shaw shook her head at her daughter and Sarah clamped her mouth shut, but still glared at Kate's father.

"Has Ann ever been on a *farm* before?" asked Grandma Shaw. She was sitting in the rocking chair beside the fire and seemed to be enjoying the scene.

Mrs. Redfeather was about to answer when Father roared, "That's enough! Ann is my new wife and you all have to accept her. That's all there is to it!"

The new Mrs. O'Carr went pale and glared at Father. "How could you not tell your children? This is just too much!"

"Yes, how could you not tell me?" Kate choked out. "This is absolutely unfair!"

"Not fair," Alex added from the sidelines. He and Ryan smiled at each other. Kate would set everything in order. She'd send Mrs. Redfeather back where she belonged.

"I don't see how it's any of your business!" Father exploded. "I've been a widower for eleven years. Isn't that long enough? Or do you want me to wait another eleven years? I had every *right* to remarry!"

"And we had every right to know!" Kate said, sobbing. She ran from the room and straight out the door.

Albert was just coming in with a basket of eggs. "Watch it, Kate!" he said, whisking the basket away from her path. But it was too late. Half a dozen eggs were cracked and one smashed to the floor.

Kate didn't even notice. She was already far out in the dooryard, with Albert staring after her.

"Really, David," said Mrs. Redfeather. "How could you? The children … you should have … I just don't believe it!"

She flounced her dark curls and bustled over to the guest bedroom, snatching her hat from the top of an old trunk as she went.

"This is starting to be fun!" Ryan whispered to Alex. "Maybe Mrs. Redfeather isn't so bad after all!"

"What's going on here?" asked Albert. "Why is Kate so upset? And who was that lady?"

"So the beautiful bride has arrived, has she?" said Mr. Shaw, entering into the house and stepping on the broken egg. He looked around the room. "Where is the new Mrs. O'Carr?"

"She's … she's …" Father waved a hand helplessly in the direction of the guest room.

"Well, what's she doing in there, David? Bring her out so we can meet her!"

Father looked flustered. Alex and Ryan had never seen him in such a state.

"Ann," Father called, "we're going to have your wedding supper. C'mon out now and join us."

"Well, let's sit down to eat," said Mr. Shaw. "My wife's been working hard all day, preparing a grand wedding feast. We mustn't disappoint her." The heavyset man plunked himself down in his chair at the end of the table with a look of complete satisfaction.

Everyone else just stood, looking at one another. Quietly, Albert left the room.

"I'm not hungry anymore," grumbled Alex. He rushed out after Albert, with Ryan in tow.

CHAPTER
FOUR

"We should've stopped this," Alex whispered loudly to Ryan.

The twins were sitting uncomfortably in an oaken pew up near the front of the Methodist Church. Kate had gotten over her shock about Father's new wife as soon as she realized it freed her to marry Albert. Albert had land and a shanty that would serve the two of them a season, until he could build a proper cabin. Father gladly granted his permission, and Kate had set about planning her wedding. The boys had never known her this way: so excited and impatient, she was almost feverish. "Like a rat leaving a sinking ship," Alex had said gloomily to Ryan, and Ryan had to agree. What had happened to the old, loyal Kate they had known and counted on all their lives?

"She's coming down the aisle in about ten minutes. It's a bit late to stop her!" whispered Ryan.

"I know, but maybe we could've stopped the circuit rider on his way from King's Town. I could've taken Duke and you could've taken Bonnie and we could've ambushed him on the road up from Bath."

"Oh, sure. But there's one problem. Father would've missed us and the horses."

"You're always thinking of ways to make more problems. Maybe we could've scared the minister with tales about pirates along the shores of Lake Ontario."

"Well, it's too late now. Look, here comes Albert ... I mean, *Bertie*!" said Ryan, rolling his eyes up to the gallery that ran around the second storey of the church.

"Yuck ... Bertie! I tell you, Ryannie, no girl is going to call me Aleckie ... ever!"

Albert Shaw stood straight and tall at the front of the clapboard church, unaware of the twins' jokes. The sun streamed through the front windows and the shadow of a maple branch played in front of the pulpit. The boys had never seen Albert look so dressed up. He was wearing knee breeches with no rips in them, a beige wool shortcoat and woollen shirt, and a flashy red cravat. But the fanciest thing was the hat he was carrying under his arm: it was made of felt and it had three corners.

"How come he needs three corners on his hat?" wondered Ryan. "Pirates have only two."

"Maybe pirates can't afford the third corner."

Ryan looked at his brother with disgust. "You sure come up with some peculiar ideas!"

Their bickering was interrupted by the sound of a small, wheezing pump organ gearing up for the opening hymn. Sarah came trooping up the aisle first in a deep pink outer petticoat and white overblouse. A pocket that should have been tucked down was flapping with every step. Alex poked Ryan and pointed to the pocket.

Ryan grabbed his hand over his mouth to keep back a snort of laughter. Just as Sarah was passing them, they looked up and saw that she didn't even notice them. She was looking over at the best man, Daniel Davis, who had recently taken her to a few barn dances. Ryan pointed.

"Looks like everybody's falling in love around here. Crazy!" said Alex, disgusted.

Not far behind Sarah came Geordie Shaw, Sarah and Albert's youngest brother. He would turn six that summer and with his white-blonde hair, he was looking angelic. It didn't help that he was carrying an embroidered cushion with the wedding ring perched on top.

"I can't stand this," said Alex. "I wouldn't be caught dead trailing up the aisle with a little pincushion and a ring."

"It's not a *pin* cushion, silly. It's a *ring* cushion."

"Same difference. All this dumb fuss so Kate can leave us and we can be stuck with that new mother and her red feathers."

"Shush, Alex, here come Father and Kate. We just gotta … "

Before the boys could do anything about it, Kate was slowly sailing down the aisle, like a white ship only much skinnier. She'd had only a month to get ready for the wedding but she was wearing a white silk dress that even Alex admitted was beautiful — made from material Ann had supplied — and their mother's white shawl. And Ann had cut Kate's hair in the new style. It used to hang down her back, but now her auburn ringlets fell only to her shoulders.

As they reached the front of the church, Father stood up. He was wearing his best grey pants and black great-coat — the outfit he'd worn just a month before at his own wedding in King's Town.

"How come only Father gets to give Kate away? She's our sister!" whispered Alex.

"Because we don't want to give her away — we want to keep her," Ryan whispered back.

Mr. Losee, the minister, began the ceremony in a deep and monotonous tone.

After a while, Alex whispered, "Know what I'm going to do when they get to the 'Speak now or forever hold your peace' part?"

"What?"

"I'm gonna stand up and tell everybody that we caught Albert kissing Kate by the stable and no one should let her marry a guy like that!" He began listening intently.

"Speak now," said the minister, "or forever … "

Alex jumped to his feet and waved one hand in the air. "I … I obj … " he managed to say before Ryan clamped his hand over Alex's mouth and pulled him back down in the pew.

A few snickers erupted from the young people seated just behind the boys, but the preacher ignored the slight interruption.

Albert put the ring onto Kate's finger and in minutes, the couple was heading back down the aisle toward the front door.

◇

Bobcat was sitting like a sphinx on a limb of a big maple tree, eyeing all the wedding guests as they poured into the dooryard of the Shaws' homestead. It was only five miles from the church — twice as close as the O'Carr farm. He was flicking his stubby tail uneasily because he knew something new was happening and he didn't know if he liked it.

The wedding feast was held out on the lawn, since it was already the end of May and the weather was unusually warm. The maples were out in new leaf and the lilac bush at the front door was in full bloom. Alex and Ryan spent most of the meal kicking each other under the table and tossing scraps of chicken to Bobcat, who made the rounds and begged from every guest. They were just about to make pirate hats out of their linen napkins when Kate and Albert appeared with their travelling bags. "I guess they're really going, aren't they?" said Ryan.

"Yeah, thanks to you tackling me back in the church."

"Well, we have to be brave and let her go."

"I don't really care," said Alex, but Ryan could see that his eyes were getting watery.

The boys ran across the yard and gave their sister a huge hug.

"We'll be coming to visit you soon," said Ryan.

"Even if we have to run away!" said Alex.

"Now, that's no talk for two big boys I've raised," said Kate. "You have to be stronger than that. Father needs you on the farm. And when you grow up to be men, you'll get Loyalist land-grants of your own."

"I know, but we'll miss you, Kate."

"Now, you be good to Ann." Kate had an uneasy feeling that the boys would start playing tricks on their stepmother once she was gone. But the rosy-cheeked Ann did not look at all concerned. She rustled over to Kate in her blue taffeta gown and gave her a bunch of lilacs.

"Come home whenever you can," said Father.

"Yes, Kate," Ann urged. "We'll look for both of you at Hay Bay in a few weeks."

"It may be longer before we're free," said Albert. "It's seeding time now, and the summer work will be upon us before we know it. We've applied for Kate's land from the British government, but haven't heard where it's to be."

"We'll have a good farm one day," said Kate, bubbling with enthusiasm at the thought of a home where she would be the real mistress.

Kate gave everyone a hug and a kiss. Alex and Ryan and Bobcat watched silently. Then Kate squatted beside Bobcat who stood firmly between her brothers. His green eyes were open wider than usual. He was standing in a restless pose, his black stripes standing out as much as ever on his grey fur.

"You're not taking Bobcat, are you?" Ryan asked fearfully. The cat's stubby ringed tail started to switch back and forth. He was angry because a big change was taking place.

Kate looked sadly at the mournful faces of her brothers.

"No, I'm not taking Bobcat," she said, "and I hope you'll take good care of him."

"Of course," said Ryan. Alex nodded his head. They were both trying hard not to cry in front of everyone.

Bobcat gave a reassuring *hummpurr* sound. "I think he's saying he'll take good care of us, the way he did that hard winter," said Ryan.

"I think so," Kate agreed, hugging each of her brothers in turn.

Then Kate climbed into the small buggy where Albert waited and they were off. For a time, Kate's head showed around the side of the buggy and she waved her arm until she was out of sight.

Bobcat gave an unearthly *meow* that made everyone turn and look at him. His black stripes stood out dark on his back, and all of his hair seemed to be standing up straight. But when the buggy disappeared from sight, Bobcat turned and walked away, his limp more noticeable than usual. He'd been like that ever since he'd been attacked while hunting food for the family in the winter of 1788. But the limp was always worse when he was tired or sad.

As the wedding guests walked back toward the house, the sun passed under a cloud and a cold breeze blew the fresh leaves on the trees. A few twigs scuttled along the ground. Alex looked over at their smiling stepmother, who was walking arm in arm with their father. She was laughing up at him and he was looking down happily at her upturned face. Alex nudged Ryan and nodded his head toward the pair.

"It's all her fault," said Alex.

"I know," said Ryan, "and we'll get even."

"You can bet on that!" said Alex.

CHAPTER
FIVE

The twins began their campaign that very day, on the way home from the wedding. As usual, Father was complaining about the state of the road. Today, he was fuming about the unworked lots belonging to the Church of England and decommissioned officers. Father always pushed the team faster as he went by these wild places.

"They're refuges for wild animals, that's what they are," grumbled Father. "A man can't pasture his cattle without losing stock to wolves and other wild creatures. And there's still too many bear attacks for civilized living."

"Still, it's beautiful," Ann replied. "Or perhaps I just think so, because the most beautiful road is the one that takes you home." She leaned her head against Father's shoulder.

"Disgusting!" mouthed the twins, both at once. Then a new light shone in Alex's eyes. He winked at his brother, and Ryan smiled widely. Sometimes, they understood each other without saying a word.

"Father!" shouted Alex. "I saw something. I swear I did!"

"Yeah," yelled Ryan. "I can smell it too! It's a bear."

Ann sat up straight. "A bear!" she said.

"Yes, just like the one that almost got Kate when we first moved here!"

"Now, Ann, it's nothing to worry about," Father said quietly. "Bears don't bother folks much if we don't bother them."

"Unless they have cubs," said Ryan. "At this time of year, it could be a mother with cubs. There's nothing wilder than a mother bear who thinks her cubs are threatened."

Alex crawled along to the front of the wagon just behind his stepmother. He had to squeeze between bags and barrels and chests, all full of wedding gifts. Some of them were Kate and Albert's — there wouldn't be room for them at first, in their tiny shanty. But most of them were from Ann's relatives in England, shipped to King's Town and forwarded to Adolphustown by Ann's father. Father hadn't had time to pick them up until yesterday.

Alex poked Ann and she jumped and turned to look down at her new stepson. "Have you ever seen a bear's claws?" he asked. "They're the size of a stump puller!" He measured about two feet with his hands.

Coming up right behind, Ryan said, "Yeah, they're mean, all right. Can tear a person to shreds with those claws, they can." He was delighted to see Ann frowning.

"That's enough, boys," said Father. "Now, Ann, I want … "

"Oh, never mind, David. I know all about bears," said Ann, turning toward the boys. "You see, when I was in King's Town, a few of us went on an overnight stay in the wilds nearby. A mother bear and two cubs were living in the woods there. A soldier who accompanied us shot the mother and then the poor cubs came right up to us. They were so forgiving. I loved those cubs all summer. But in the fall, my father said I had to let them go."

"You did that?" asked Ryan.

"I don't believe it!" said Alex.

"Alex!" Father roared.

"Now, David, Alex has a right to his opinions. Not too many folks believed it even when they saw them. I called the cubs Sam and Sack. They even got to know their own names. They followed me around all summer, so now, I can almost talk bear language. I doubt any bear would attack me!"

Father made a sound that was almost a groan. "Don't be too sure of that, Ann." Now, *he* looked worried.

"You can?" asked Ryan. "You can talk bear language? Really?" There was admiration in his tone, but Alex refused to sound even interested.

"I've heard enough about bears," Father grumbled. He was in one of his moods, so the boys knew they'd better go back to their spot. For now, their games would have to stop.

Alex tapped Ryan on the shoulder. They crawled over and around the bags and barrels again and reached the back of the wagon.

"She may be all right, after all," said Ryan.

"I'm not so sure," said Alex. "I think she's making up a lot of stuff — just to impress Father."

"Maybe," said Ryan, "but I sort of believe her. You know,

Alex, I'd like to have a baby bear."

"Bobcat would never stand for it," Alex said scornfully. He hoped Ryan wasn't getting soft on him, and forgetting their pact to make life difficult for Ann. He decided to give his brother the silent treatment the rest of the way. Ryan gave him a look or two, but Alex's only response was to glare at Ann's back, as if to say, "It's her fault."

All unaware, Ann smiled at the boys as Father helped her down from the wagon. "Home again, home again, jiggety jig," she said.

Even Ryan had to roll his eyes at that. Nursery rhymes! What did Ann think they were, babies? Then, when Father opened the door and Ann looked around the spacious kitchen with a sigh, Alex caught her look of satisfaction.

The cat who swallowed the cream, he thought in disgust, and saw in Ryan's face that his twin had come to the same conclusion.

"You know, Ann," said Father. "I was thinking that with Kate gone, you could make that second loft room into a sewing room."

"A *sewing* room …?" Ryan said right out loud, wrinkling his nose, but Father ignored him. Ryan gaped at Alex. How could Father give away *Kate's* room!

"What'll Kate do when she visits, then?" demanded Alex. "And what about Bobcat? He sleeps there sometimes."

"Oh, I wouldn't take Kate's room," said Ann. "But I was thinking about a parlour to entertain all your friends, David. Don't you want a …?"

But Father was already shaking his head. "I'm too

busy for that right now, Ann—getting the land ready and seeding and all. But I'll build you a grand parlour at the other side of the kitchen when the year's work is done. Yes, my dear, you'll have your parlour after harvest time. Maybe the boys and I will get it framed in after spring seeding."

The boys looked at each other and then at the late-afternoon sky. They knew there would be work, work, and more work ahead of them for months to come.

"Humph," said Alex.

"You never had time to build *Kate* a parlour," said Ryan.

"All right, boys, that's enough. Now hop to it, and unload the wagon. Take the smaller things off first. I'll take the barrels, and you can help me with the trunk."

Father moved to the side of the wagon, rolled a barrel onto his shoulder and headed toward the front door.

The boys looked at their father with admiration. He might be grumpy sometimes, but he sure was strong and determined.

"Give yourself a few years, boys, and you'll be lifting such weight and more," said a familiar voice behind them. Both boys turned around like lightning. There was the Mohawk man who'd saved their father's life during the Hungry Year. He still hunted in these parts, and he'd been taking care of the O'Carrs' cows and pigs and chickens while they were away. Although it was close to fifteen miles to Deseronto, the Mohawk reserve, where Tówi and his family lived, Tówi often cut across country through the woods.

"Baron!" Alex shouted as their collie dog bounded up behind Tówi. Baron was the son of the Shaws' dog, Rover.

"Tówi!" Father boomed. "More than good to see you! Any problems with the animals?"

"No, nothing to be concerned about … but you might have some trouble getting your dog back. Baron here has been following me everywhere."

"Well, we'll just put out some good food for him. That should bring him back." Baron was a big friendly dog, who liked to eat.

"You can try!" Tówi laughed. "And I'll do my best to ignore him!"

"Speaking of food," said Ann, "I need to get supper going — and I need some time to plan what kind of cake I'm going to bake for the boys tomorrow." She smiled at the twins, but they just gave her cold stares and pretended not to hear. Then they turned tail and shuffled off toward the old shanty they'd lived in when they'd first come to Hay Bay. Bobcat was jumping down from its roof. He always made it home from the Shaws before they did.

The late afternoon sun sent shafts of dusty light through the shanty's one tiny window.

"The trouble is, Ann *does* know how to bake," said Ryan, flopping down on a sack of grain beside Bobcat. He was feeling a little hungry and there was no point passing up good cooking.

"Not like our Kate!" said Alex, plunking himself down on a pickle barrel.

Ryan kept silent. Privately, he felt Ann's cooking was a vast improvement on Kate's. And as far as he knew,

Kate had never made a cake in her life.

"Meowwww!" cried Bobcat. He sounded sad. The cat's limp was evident as he prowled around the room.

Ryan ruffled Bobcat's black-striped coat.

"He misses Kate," said Alex. "Maybe he'll go find her at her and Albert's new place. I've heard of cats walking miles and miles to get back home!"

"But he *is* home, and he still has us," said Ryan.

"You know what I mean." Alex's brow was furrowed. "I've been thinking — we can't do much to bring Kate back, now that she's married and all, but I bet we can make things so unpleasant for *you know who*, she'll pack her bags and go back to King's Town."

"Her *bags*!" both boys shouted out. They'd forgotten all about Father's orders. And they knew they couldn't get away with outright disobedience. They bolted for the one door of the little cabin and just made it through without knocking each other over.

Then they ran to the wagon — only to find that Ann's bags were all gone. "Did Father …?" Alex gasped.

"No, he didn't," said a woman's firm voice behind them.

"Did *you*?" asked Ryan.

"Yes. But don't concern yourselves. I would have liked some help, but it's all right."

"Where are *our* bags?" asked Ryan.

"Oh, I took them in, too," said Ann. "They're in your room."

"You mean you got up that ladder with our bags?" asked Alex.

"Of course. Do you think I can't climb a ladder?"

"No, but … "

"We thought you were a lady something or other. Ladies don't climb ladders."

"My mother was a lady, but not I." Ann shook her head firmly. "Mother grew up in a fine house with servants, but most of my life has been spent in army camps with Mother, who followed Father all over with his work."

"As an army surgeon?"

"Yes."

"Did he ever take you to help?"

"Yes, a few times."

"What could you do?"

"Hold a sick soldier's hand."

"Does Father know about that?" said Alex, eyes narrowed. He was planning to tell Father right away. Ann seemed to be bragging and he would certainly let Father know.

"Why did you hold soldiers' hands?" Ryan asked.

"Well, one was a patient of Father's. I poured whisky down the young man's throat and then … "

"Why did you give him whisky?" asked Alex, eager now to hear the rest. He was sure that Father would not like this tale.

"Well, the poor fellow had blood poisoning in his leg. So Father sawed it off just below the knee!"

Ryan almost choked. "He did *what*?"

"He would have died if he'd kept that leg."

"Did he get better?"

"Oh, yes, he had a wooden leg after that. But his dancing days were over."

Alex wanted to hear more. "Did you help with other patients, too?"

"Lots of times. But I think we'd better go inside now. I want to unpack."

"Are you going to take over Kate's room?" asked Ryan anxiously.

"No, but I might work on a new quilt up there sometimes. You wouldn't mind that, would you?"

"I might," said Ryan, "but ... I suppose ... Kate wouldn't mind."

"Our Kate was always letting us go into her room, but then that's different — we're her brothers!" Alex boasted.

"I know," said Ann. "She's your sister and your mother all in one."

"That's true," said Ryan, "and it's going to be mighty lonely around here without her."

"Well, you have me," said Ann cheerily. "I'm not Kate but ... " She hesitated. The boys were staring at her coldly. For a while, they'd thought she understood. Now they knew she didn't. She could never replace Kate. Ann looked back at them with pleading eyes.

The boys looked the other way to hide their own pain. Ann would never be like Kate to them. It was not possible.

"Here it is!" said Ann, holding up the cake. Alex had to admit it looked like a normal cake, but he knew better. He gave Ryan a sly look. Then they both looked innocently at Father. He was going to have a big surprise!

That very afternoon, the twins had switched the labels on the small tin containers where Ann kept her salt and sugar. Then they'd taken salt out of the big bag stored in the back pantry and poured it into the larger sugar container.

They watched Ann like two young hawks as she cut four huge pieces and slid them onto her best china plates. The plates were a wedding present from her mother's mother. As she handed out a piece to Father first, the boys' eyes met and the corners of their mouths twitched.

"We sure do appreciate your wonderful baking, Ann," said Father, "eh, boys?"

Alex and Ryan picked up their forks, but they didn't touch the cake. They'd let Father be the one to complain. They watched him take a big mouthful. He opened his eyes wide and the twins nearly laughed out loud. But they weren't prepared for what happened next.

"That's wonderful cake, Ann," Father said. "The best I've ever tasted."

Alex dropped his fork on the floor and Ryan coughed to cover up his shock. So Father was going to pretend. That meant that everyone would have to eat this cake and pretend, too. The twins almost choked at the thought. Ryan took a small piece first and tried to wash it down with a drink of milk. Then Alex took a mouthful and chewed it as slowly as possible.

Father wasn't pretending! The cake was good!

"Thank you, dear," said Ann. "How do *you* like the cake, boys?"

"Fine," Alex mumbled.

Ryan just nodded. He was going for another mouthful.

"You know, David," said Ann, studying the boys closely. "The funniest thing happened today. I almost mixed up the salt and sugar. It must have happened yesterday, when I was filling my tins from the sacks. Today, when I scooped out my cake ingredients, I just couldn't resist sticking my finger in the sugar. And I positively gagged. It was salt! Sure enough, I had filled those containers with the opposite ingredients. Would you believe that? Just think what would have happened if I hadn't found out what I had done."

The boys kept eating.

"Good job you have a sweet tooth," said Father.

"A sugar finger," said Ann, staring straight at Alex and Ryan. The look was not lost on them. They were squirming on their bench.

"Never heard of a sugar finger before," Alex grumbled.

"Nor me," said Ryan. "But this is good cake."

Ann smiled at Ryan and he smiled back, but Alex was still scowling. The cake hadn't changed *his* mood.

Father finished his cake in no time and was soon drinking his after-supper cup of tea. "Well, boys, we must get a move on and get to bed. Tomorrow, we have to pull stumps out of that extra field that I'm clearing this year. I want to have an even bigger crop." Ever since the hard winter, Father was afraid they'd run out of food again. So he kept adding more fields and planting more crops. Father was a slave driver at the best of times, but now all he ever thought about was work. The boys knew there was another reason, too. Their new stepmother wanted things that Kate never got — like a parlour. They hated her even more for that.

"Now, David. Don't work too hard. Forget about my parlour," said Ann. "It can wait till fall." She wasn't looking at Father though. She was looking at the twins.

Alex and Ryan couldn't believe their ears. Ann always seemed to know what they were thinking!

It might be harder to drive her away than they thought.

PART TWO

Alex and the Pirates

CHAPTER
SIX

"I won't bring your bucket!" shouted Alex. "It's not my turn. It's yours!"

"That's not fair. I brought your water yesterday," Ryan shot back. "Now it's your turn!"

"Go jump in the bay, Ryan," said Alex. "That was yesterday. I've been doing lots of things for you since then. Besides, you're closer. So bring it!"

Duke whinnied and Bonnie shifted in her traces, jolting the wagon forward.

"Hold on, Bonnie!" Alex yelled as he stomped up the steep slope, lugging his bucket.

It was mid-August of 1793 and the boys were frying in the heat of another dry summer. Father and Ann had gone to a barn-raising nearby, but the twins had to stay home to water the growing corn.

"I don't see why we couldn't have gone to help build the barn," Alex grumbled.

"Yeah," growled Ryan. "Ann got to go. I pity the men when they taste her roast chicken!"

Back in June, when Kate and Albert had come for

supper, Ann had left a few insides behind, and the roast chicken had been a disaster. The evening had been a disaster in other ways as well. Ryan and Alex couldn't get a word in edgewise, the way their sister and stepmother chattered on. Now that she was married, Kate seemed no better than all the other old wives. There was a suspicious amount of whispering over the dishes, too, as well as looks in the twins' direction. Then, before she and "Bertie" left, Kate took the boys aside.

"Now, boys!" Kate said, looking stern. "This tomfoolery has got to stop."

The boys tried to look as if they didn't know what she was talking about.

"You have got to behave. No more playing pranks on Ann."

"She's a tattletale," said Ryan.

"Yeah!" said Alex.

Kate shook her head. "I know you boys, and I had my suspicions. I made her tell me."

The boys grimaced.

"I mean it. It should be obvious by now that Ann means to stay. You should give her some credit — a lesser woman would have been long gone, the way you two carry on!"

Kate laughed, then, and hugged them both tight.

"Promise you'll be good to her," she whispered, and they did. What else could they do? Kate was still their sister, and they still loved her — even if she was leaving them in Ann's clutches again.

Alex sat down and leaned against a big cottonwood beside his brother. They both stared across the bay.

"Why do you want to fight over these silly buckets?" said Ryan, smiling. "Father won't know how much we've watered — as long as the dust is settled. We can quit right now!" He stretched out under the tree. It was too hot to fight.

"Hey, Ryan," Alex said. "Let's go for a swim." He stared at his brother, who had closed his eyes. Ryan was still and his blond hair was wet with the sweat that fell across his brow.

"Ryan?" Alex cried. "Are you awake? Hey … you're not asleep! Quit pretending!"

Alex ran a leaf across Ryan's nose trying to make it feel like a fly. Ryan brushed the leaf away. Then he opened one eye, squinted up at Alex, and moved his lips to form the word "no."

"I'll go by myself then," said Alex. He jumped up, energetic in spite of the heat.

As Alex walked slowly down the steep path to the shoreline, he recalled that it was somewhere around here where his father had fallen and broken his leg, during the Hungry Year. He could remember a little about it, but not much. Mostly, he remembered Kate telling them about it over and over again. Reaching the shore of the bay, he began tearing off his clothes.

He stripped off his brown wool breeches and then flung his long-tailed linen shirt on top. Without looking back he waded into the warm water and plunged happily along up to his waist. That water felt so good. The farther he went, the better he felt. Father was crazy not to let them swim alone. It was just a dip, and Alex knew he'd work much faster once he was cooled down.

He waded out a short distance, then flung himself farther into the fresh, cool water. He was careful not to go too far out but swam parallel to the shore. His wet hair clung to his head and over his eyes. He hit a sandbar and staggered to his feet, brushing the hair away.

Then, all of a sudden, a vicious wave hit full force across his back. The white foam bubbled around him. He sputtered, choked, and coughed. But his head was above the wave again in a few seconds, and he bobbed around, enjoying the motion. This was great!

Alex reached another shallow spot just as another wave hit him. He took the impact more easily this time. Delighted, Alex watched for more waves, diving over them, swimming under them, or simply going limp and letting them carry him along. He thought a wind down on Lake Ontario must be washing the waves into Hay Bay. That was unusual. Maybe a storm was coming.

At last he drifted back into the shallows and started wading to shore. As he came closer, he scratched his head in consternation. Was this the shoreline he'd left behind? It seemed different, and there was no sign of his clothes! Well, he was pretty certain he'd been swimming north, and he hadn't gone far. He'd find his way back all right, but he'd feel silly walking along the shore with nothing on.

"Ryan, Ryan," he yelled. Then he heard a low rumble of thunder in the distance. Maybe that would wake Ryan up.

Alex stayed in water up to his chest as he scanned the

shrubs on shore. That way no one coming by would notice that he'd lost his clothes. Then he laughed at himself. Who but Ryan, and maybe Father, would come this way? Well, there was Ann — but he'd have to risk it. He was getting chilly.

Alex splashed to his feet, shivering. He had to find his things. "Ryan!" he called. "Did you take my clothes?"

He waited for a moment, then made the owl call. But his twin did not answer. All Alex could hear were the waves slopping against the shore and the thunder rumbling in the distance. A gusty wind was blowing from the water to the shore now, and splashing foaming water against his ankles.

Just then his breeches went sailing by. "Ohhh!" he gasped as he ran through the shallow water after them. He must catch his breeches! He couldn't let them float away. Every time he reached out to grasp them, the wind whipped them away. The wind seemed to be playing a game with him.

He was on dry land now, but there was no one in sight, so he laughed out loud. He was enjoying the game. Father would punish him, though, if he saw him running around in his birthday suit. But the thought made him laugh even louder. He could picture the shocked look on his stepmother's face if they all came home about now and went looking for him and his brother.

Then Alex's luck improved. He came to a place along the shore that was filled with green, swaying reeds. His breeches were sitting on top of a bunch of them at the water's edge. He had to wade out a few feet to snag them, but he got there and held the old things high above the water as he waded back to shore through the mud and stones. Then he pulled them up over his knees and to his waist. This was fine. He didn't need his shirt though he wished he had his boots.

Alex plopped down on the grass and sat with elbows on his knees. Now that he was on shore, he had an idea of where he was. Before going back to Ryan, he'd explore.

Just as he was deciding where to go, two men appeared, walking along the shoreline, just the other side of a patch of reeds. They were swinging buckets at their sides. Funny, he hadn't noticed them before they got this close. They must be from a bateau docked just around the bend.

One man had curly red hair all over his chest; the other had thick black hair and a black beard and bushy moustache. Lopsided straw hats were pulled down low enough to shade their eyes. Alex figured you could tell a lot more when you looked a fellow straight in the eye, but he didn't want to get that close. So he jumped up, planning to run back to the wagon. Who were these men anyway?

"Hey, boy," one of them shouted. "Where can we get some spring water?" It was too late.

Alex turned around and stared at the black-haired fellow. He'd pushed his hat back off his forehead and was looking straight at Alex. Despite his bushy black eyebrows and thick moustache, he didn't look too intimidating.

"A shilling if you show us a spring-fed stream," said the red-haired man.

"Well, mister," Alex drawled, trying to appear confident. "I can show you to the freshest stream this side of heaven, but I'm wondering this. Was that a shilling each or a shilling between the two of you?"

The sailor with the mop of black hair laughed loudly. That was a merry laugh if Alex had ever heard one. These fellows seemed all right.

"I reckon we've come across a real businessman, Ivan," said the black-haired man.

Alex smiled back at him and slowed his pace. The distance between them was shortening.

"One shilling will have to do, since that's all we have," growled Ivan, the red-haired man. *Reminds me of Father,* Alex thought.

When they reached the stream, the men fell on their knees and drank straight from the water. "It's good, all right," said the dark-haired one. "We'd better pay the kid." Alex held out his hand and smiled as a coin dropped into it.

"Mighty pleased to help you, gentlemen," he said. "It would be my privilege to see you back to your bateau, as well."

Alex waited hopefully while the two men filled their buckets. When they were done, they didn't say anything, but turned and walked briskly away. *Well, they didn't say no,* Alex thought, and trotted after them.

The black-haired man turned. "Tag along if you've a mind to," he said. Then he fell back in step with Alex. "What's your name, boy?"

"Alex. Well, it's really Alexander Berton, but the family

calls me Alex, for short." He was up walking between the two men now. "I had a grandfather named Alex. I was named after him. My twin was named Ryan Benjamin after another grand —"

"We don't have time for your whole family history, boy," barked Ivan, who was striding on ahead.

"Don't mind him," said the black-haired man. "It's a hot day. I'm James."

"Very pleased to meet you," said Alex.

"That sure was a grand creek of fresh water," James continued. "Reminded me of home."

"Where's home?" Alex asked. He'd hoped to find out more about these men, but he hadn't dared to ask till now.

"Better you don't know," said James.

"Why?" Alex asked. This could be the beginning of an adventure! But James did not answer. He just strode on in silence.

After about fifteen minutes, the full bateau came into view. It was a beauty! It had great sails, which another two men were starting to unfurl. The craft bobbed up and down on the waves and the white sails looked brilliant in the hot summer sun.

"How did you ever get a huge boat this far?" Alex asked as he stepped boldly across the rough log serving as a gangplank. Four wooden benches stretched from one side of the bateau to the other. A load of barrels stood between them in the centre.

Three more men on deck stared openly at Alex. They did not look friendly.

"Where'd you pick up that stray?" said one sailor.

"Have you lost your senses?" growled a mean-looking grey-haired fellow. Alex thought he might be the captain, since he seemed accustomed to barking out orders. A many-coloured scarf tied around his neck blew out around him. It must have been almost three feet long.

Alex stepped down into the bateau after Ivan and James, dodging barrels and crates but keeping up with them as they headed toward the man with the grey hair.

"This boy led us to the fresh water," James explained. "This here is Captain Gordon," he added, to Alex.

"Mighty pleased to meet you, sir." Alex figured he'd better remember his manners. These men looked dangerous. The captain grunted and nodded his head slightly before he turned back to watch the men unfurl the sails.

"Well, there's not much to see once you get here," said James. "And now you've seen it, you'd best get off before we use our poles to push out to deep water."

"Where are you headed, mister?" Alex asked. The captain and his men turned and glared at their young visitor. Two large dark clouds rolled across the sky and cast an eerie gloom over the sailors.

"Oh, I don't know," said James. "We're just out having a good time."

Alex didn't answer. But he wasn't *that* stupid! People often came this way in canoes, but few bateaux passed by unless they were crowded with immigrants.

"Well," Alex drawled, trying to sound tough, "how about taking a poor, bored boy for a sail in your bateau?"

"No time," said James firmly, stroking his beard and shaking his head.

"Oh, you could just take me around the bend with you, then let me off. I can make my own way back," Alex assured the man. "I know this countryside like the back of my hand. After all, we've been in this neighbourhood for six years."

"Oldtimers, eh?" James said. "Loyalists?"

"Yes, sir," said Alex. "But we came too late. All that was left was land full of trees and underbrush. We have to work like slaves. When I grow up, I don't want to be a farmer. I want to be a hunter ... or maybe a sailor!"

"You want to have the idle life of a sailor, do you? Is that why you were swimming in the middle of the day?" asked James, a smile making his moustache twitch.

"No!" Alex protested. He'd suddenly remembered he should be feeling guilty for going swimming and leaving Ryan.

"Well, why were you swimming all by yourself, then?"

"My father and stepmother went to help our neighbours build a barn. My brother and I were left alone at our place."

"I see." James's eyes were twinkling. "While the cat's away, the mice will play." Then he laughed and turned to the captain. "This fellow wants to go with us for a little sail — just round yonder bend. It would be no trouble to drop him there."

The captain scowled again, but said nothing. So Alex sat down and watched the great white sails. They were unfurled even farther now, and they were waving lightly in the breeze. The smells of tar and weathered ropes filled the air.

"You know, Alex," said James, looking down on him from under his black eyebrows. "Sometimes, it's hard to stop this here sailing boat. You might have a long walk home."

"It would be worth it!" Alex said cheerily. "I've got all day!"

When the bateau started to move, Alex sat down on a bench in the middle. His foot hit a cask that was hard as rock, tucked underneath him. *Were these casks holding supplies for new immigrants?* Alex wondered. Then a strange feeling came over him. Army officers usually brought supplies to the settlers, and these men weren't dressed in anything like uniforms. They didn't sound British, either, as all the soldiers and sailors usually did. They sounded like Americans, and looked like …

Pirates! Now, he knew who these men were. It all made sense. *They were pirates!*

Suddenly, Alex changed his mind about this ride. But the bateau had left shore and was headed out of the bay and into Lake Ontario.

CHAPTER
SEVEN

The August air was hot and close, but Alex was shivering. Of course, Alex said to himself, he wasn't shivering because he was afraid of these men. It was just that the wind was stronger farther out on the water. He couldn't wait to get home to tell Ryan he'd met some real pirates — if he got home alive, that is!

"What're you staring at, boy?" asked Ivan. The grumpy red-haired pirate shook his head and turned to James. "Lost your senses, you have, bringing him aboard."

"What's the matter, Alex?" James asked, sounding as friendly as ever. "Are you feeling a little seasick?"

Alex stared up into James's twinkling eyes. For a pirate, he was a nice fellow. "Nothing's wrong," he said. "It's been a grand ride. But I'll be getting out around the corner. I don't want to walk for two days to get home!"

"Ship to starboard," yelled a sailor from his post halfway up the mast. He was holding a spyglass to his eye. "Almost at the entrance to this bay."

"Unfurl the sails — all the way," the captain yelled. "Put your backs into it, men! We'll not wait to be blocked in."

James left Alex and grabbed one of the oars. All the sailors except the man on watch were rowing or steering the boat. Alex saw the distance between them and the shore getting wider and wider.

"Where is she now?" the captain shouted.

"No closer! Maybe she didn't see us."

"We can't count on that. Keep the sails unfurled."

"But what about me?" Alex stepped over to James and poked him in the shoulder. "I don't want to go on a voyage, James. I want to go back." Alex wasn't a worrier by nature, but he was getting anxious now. Ryan would be wondering where he was, and Father and Ann would be coming home soon. They would all be furious when they discovered he was gone.

James turned to Alex. "Don't worry. We'll get you home sometime, but it won't be right now. As soon as we dare stop, I'll have the men turn in toward the shore. You did say you know this whole area."

"Yes, I do," Alex bragged untruthfully. "But it's too hot to walk far."

James sighed. "Captain, do you think you could dock around the bend — just long enough to drop Alex off?" he asked.

"No! I don't want to risk it! Not now. Keep going!" The captain's mouth was curled into a nasty grimace and his eyes were squinting into narrow slits as he stared to the eastern horizon.

Just then the bateau lurched sideways, hit by a huge wave. Alex sat down with a thud. This was just the kind of excitement he liked, but he hadn't expected to be kidnapped! He stared in horror as high, white-capped waves hit the bateau one after another, moving it farther and farther from shore. The boat tipped from side to side, nearly turning over. Then, an even bigger wave washed over them all. Alex spit the water from his mouth just in time to see another foaming wave coming straight at him.

Alex's heart raced. He was sure the bateau would soon be toppling over. "James, James!" he shouted through the spray. "James!"

The entire crew struggled with the rigging and the oars as the waves continued to slap against the boat. No one even looked in his direction. Alex clutched the sides of the bench, frozen with fear.

"They're gaining on us!" James shouted to the captain. Turning, Alex could barely see the topsails of a ship through the spray. They were still quite far in the distance, but visible.

The captain strained to see through his spyglass. "Yes, I believe it's the British military. But we aren't beaten yet. Head around the land. We'll go for the inlet."

Alex was sure now. These men were pirates. *American* pirates, in double trouble because they were in Canadian waters. And he, Alex O'Carr, was in triple trouble. He would be caught right in the middle! He wondered uneasily if the pirates had been Revolutionaries as well. Father hadn't been a Loyalist, officially — but he'd sheltered a few spies and couriers. Perhaps it was a good thing James and Ivan hadn't wanted to hear his family history!

"We're almost around the bend and then we'll be hidden from view. It'll take us another half-hour to reach the inlet, but we'll be safe there, and the water'll be calmer," said the captain.

"Calm — till they catch us, that is!" yelled Ivan, who had not stopped rowing the whole time.

"And we'll be trapped!" James turned away from his work on the sails.

"I have plans," the captain said calmly. "To starboard, there!"

The bateau moved slowly around, then cut into the waves, and before long, it had turned sharply around a bend and was sailing straight ahead. Alex was glad to see that land was still in sight, but he wondered why they weren't heading for shore right away. One thing he did know, however: if the bateau capsized out here, he would not be able to swim to shore — not through those white-capped waves. He doubted if any of the sailors would be able to make it to shore either. So why were they staying so far out in the water?

"She's moving faster now," said the captain. "Another twenty to thirty minutes, fellows, and we'll be in the inlet. Hang in there!"

"This wind's a godsend," said Ivan. "It'll move us along much faster."

Move us along where? Alex wondered. He couldn't see anything but forest along the shore, so the settled farms must be farther inland. He knew they were going around the Prince Edward County peninsula. But this shoreline did not look familiar.

Still, the waves were not hitting the bateau as fiercely now, and the oarsmen were not rowing as furiously. But James was still frowning and looking back.

"James, when are we …?"Alex began to ask, but James did not appear to hear him. He was helping another sailor adjust the larger sail. Alex sighed. He might just as well save his breath.

So they sailed on and on. No one paid any attention to the boy seated on the bench across the middle of the bateau. And the more time passed, the more Alex wished he was back with Ryan. He'd wanted more excitement, but this was too much. How would he ever find his way back home?

Just when Alex thought the boat ride would last forever, the bateau took a sharp turn into a sheltered inlet. Land now surrounded them on three sides, and they appeared to be sailing straight for the farthest point inland.

Alex heaved a sigh of relief. The waters were still choppy, but this area was much safer. Straight ahead of them, a sandy beach was closed in by dense woods.There were many thick green maples and solid oak trees beside stands of weeping willows. Alex was wet to the skin, but he didn't mind. Soon they would be ashore.

But Alex's relief was short-lived. A silence had settled on the men as they caught their breath. Then James spoke to the captain.

"Well, how long do you figure we have before they over-take us?"

"A half-hour, maybe a bit more, before they turn into the inlet. But they'll not be able to sail into the channel—

not with that big ship. They'll sink anchor at the entrance. Still, we'll have to move fast, men. Use the poles and steer her to the farthest point in. Then we'll climb out and make for those trees. They'll be our cover."

"Then what?" asked the sailor who was steering the bateau.

"We'll bury the gold and burn the bateau," said the captain.

The men gasped.

"You'll what?" yelled Ivan.

"You got a better idea?" James turned and faced his fellow sailors. "If they catch us with the gold, they'll hang us for sure. If the bateau is burned, they'll know we took to the woods in an uninhabited area. They're professional sailors, not woodsmen. They might get lost hunting for us."

"Yeah," growled Ivan. "I know how they feel."

The bateau was now close to land. The sailors lifted their poles out of the bateau and into the water, touching bottom. Then they began pushing the boat toward the shore.

"Leave the sails hanging," said the captain. "They'll burn faster that way."

"They may be too wet to burn," said Ivan.

"We'll use the gunpowder," said the captain. "It won't leave much behind. Move over, boy, till I get that cask." Alex shuddered as the captain reached under him. *He'd been sitting on top of the gunpowder!* That's what the rock-hard cask had been holding!

In an amazingly short time, the bateau was beached

and the men began scrambling over the side and into the water. Still on the bateau, Ivan hoisted a casket only two feet from Alex to the side of the boat. He tipped it over the edge, and three men caught it. Next, he threw three shovels toward the shore.

The men waded back a piece and began digging. The sand was soft, and water kept filling the hole as they dug.

"The waves'll wash away any signs of the digging," said the captain, who had hardly taken his eyes away from his spyglass and the outer waves of Lake Ontario. Alex was looking out, too, and could see no sign of the ship.

Almost half an hour passed before the casket was lowered deep into its watery hole. As the men were piling the last shovelfuls of wet sand over the hidden gold, the captain yelled, "Now, pull the bateau farther inland and over here." He pointed to the east about thirty feet. Grunting, the men pulled and strained to get the boat on shore.

"We'll go separately, men," the captain said, "so if they do decide to track us, some of us will have a chance. Each of you take as much as you can carry — muskets and powder, and traps and fishing gear. Unless, of course, you want to beg for food from the farmers."

The men laughed at the idea. Alex couldn't understand why. Settlers were always willing to share, even with pirates, and there was plenty to eat this time of year. Thinking about food made his stomach rumble. He stood there helplessly while the men climbed into the bateau and took their spoil.

James handed Alex a bucket filled with pans and gear.

"Here, take these. We'll be travelling together." That was a relief. Then Alex looked at his bare feet and wondered how he could possibly run over all the pine cones and brush in the woods that lay ahead.

"I can't go in there in my *bare feet*," he said.

James looked, too, then climbed back onto the bateau. He grabbed some deerskin from under the seat and shoved it into Alex's already-loaded bucket. Again, James returned to the bateau. He came out this time with both arms full — with a fish net, a musket, another bucket, and a frayed topcoat which he put on quickly.

Alex watched as the captain said goodbye to his fellow pirates, then headed back to the bateau.

"C'mon, Alex!" said James. "Run for it! We don't want to be around when the bateau explodes!"

"But maybe," Alex stammered, "I should wait for the British ship." After all, he wasn't a pirate or an American. The British officers would know that as soon as Alex opened his mouth.

"Don't fool yourself. You've got an American accent just like us. They're bound to believe the worst."

Alex stared at James in surprise. "I don't have an accent," he said.

"Well, you don't sound British, anyway," said James.

Alex scratched his head. James was right. He sure didn't talk like Ann, and she was definitely British. He must have got his so-called accent from Kate and his father.

Still, Father had known some British officers. Maybe ...

Bang! Smoke and the heavy smell of sulphur rose into the air, smothering the fresh tang of water and trees.

Alex's ears rang. The captain had fallen flat about twenty feet behind them. James ran back and helped the man to his feet. Soon, the two were up and running. As they ran past Alex, James yelled, "Do as you like, but you may be in danger. The sailors might force you aboard as a deckhand. A hard life, my boy."

All at once, Alex knew what he wanted. He wanted to be back home with Ryan, back at Hay Bay. He ran to the edge of the thick green woods, then turned for one last look at the inlet and the burning ship. Just beyond the smoke, he could see a vessel more than four times the size of the bateau nosing its way around the corner and facing into the inlet. Had it sunk anchor there?

All the pirates but James had disappeared, now, and his friend stood alone at the edge of the woods. He waved an arm above his head, motioning Alex to follow.

"They're coming, James! Wait for me!" he shouted. "I don't want to be a deckhand."

CHAPTER
EIGHT

Alex ran like a rabbit, without even feeling his bare feet hit the stones and roots between the sand banks and the edge of the forest. Entering the woods, Alex had to slow down, making his way more carefully through the tangled undergrowth. James led the way, pulling back branches and vines as they crept ahead.

As they walked along slowly, the pain hit Alex. He looked down at his feet. Even in the dim light of the thick bush, he could see that his feet were bleeding. Stumbling along behind James in silence, he could hide his pain no longer.

"James," he gasped. "My feet!" He collapsed on the ground and leaned against a tree.

"I'm sorry," James said, turning back. "I forgot you had no boots. I can make you moccasins from that deerskin tonight, but there's no time now."

Alex gritted his teeth and they started off again, but they were moving more slowly. He was glad to see James glancing back once in a while, for he felt he was going to drop at any minute. Finally, he tripped over a root and crumpled onto the ground, trying not to sob.

James came back, picked him up, and flopped him over his shoulder. How embarrassing! Alex was eleven and almost a man, and here he was being carried like a sack of potatoes by a burly pirate! But his feet hurt so badly now, he didn't object. The motion of moving began to make him feel drowsy.

"Wake up, boy," James growled, "and hang on. I have my hands full of gear. I can't carry a dead weight too!" Alex woke himself up and wrapped both legs around the man's waist and his arms around his neck, but he kept nodding off to sleep.

Finally, James stopped and flung Alex down. The boy hit the ground with a thud and sat up feeling like a mass of bruises.

"They won't catch us now," said James. "They're probably still digging through the remains of the bateau. They wanted the gold, not us."

Alex had a horrible thought. "When they don't find the gold, won't they think we brought it with us?"

"Yes, but we've had a good head start. And we're travelling with a real woodsman, don't forget." James smiled.

Alex was about to ask, "Who?" when he realized whom James meant. "Uh, James ... "

James laughed. "I reckon you're about to tell me you don't know as much as you claimed, is that right?"

Alex was relieved he didn't have to spell it out.

"Never mind, son. I have an idea of where I'm going. Between the two of us, we'll manage," James assured the boy. "Now it's time we settled for the night."

Together they cut some fir branches and made a couple of rough beds.

"You rest for now," James told Alex. "I'm going to make your moccasins while there's still some light." His voice was low and firm. He sounded just like Father.

Alex wondered what his family was doing now. Father would be really angry that he'd taken off and left Ryan with all the chores. Probably, Kate would be worried that a bear might find him. She always worried about bears. Ann ... Ann wouldn't be worried exactly, since Alex wasn't her own boy. But she might be baking up a storm. One thing Ann seemed to know about was a boy's stomach. She'd know how hungry an adventure like this could make a fellow. Of course, after he'd eaten, Ann would fill up the tub and make him scrub his skin off. She was far too fond of washing. She'd been making the twins take a bath once a week since she came, whether they were dirty or not!

As his stomach grumbled, Alex worried that someone on shore back at Hay Bay had seen him sailing out to Lake Ontario with the pirates. Everyone in Adolphustown and Fredericksburgh would know that he, Alex O'Carr, had run away from home to become a pirate! His reputation would be ruined forever!

Alex missed Ryan the most, of course. Ryan would be going crazy wondering what happened to him. And what would Ryan do if he didn't get back in one piece? They were twins, after all, so even though they got angry with each other from time to time, they were also best friends. Ryan was probably even thinking about him at this very minute!

"Please, God," Alex prayed, "let Ryan know I'm on my way home. Tell him I'm sorry I took off. I'm coming home, Ryan, I'm coming home!"

"What's that you say?" James asked, but Alex didn't answer. There was no point. James wouldn't understand. No one understood about twins.

◇

"Wake up!"

Someone was clutching Alex's shoulder in a firm grip and shaking him. He blinked his eyes open and stared straight up into James's dark brown eyes.

"We can't waste good daylight," said James, crouching over Alex and thrusting something into his hand. "Here, eat this cheese and bread."

Alex really woke up then. "This isn't enough to keep a bird alive," he grumbled as he sat up.

"Is that all you got to say, boy?"

"Thanks," said Alex, chomping on the scrap of cheese. He guessed he better mind his manners or James might leave him there in the middle of the woods. It might take him a while to find his way out alone.

James threw the pair of newly sewn moccasins on the ground in front of Alex. His mouth still full, Alex grabbed them and slipped them on quickly. They felt firm and comfortable. He held up one foot and saw that they had double soles. On his sore feet, they felt even better than stiff boots.

"Well, mister," said Alex, beaming, "I sure appreciate these great moccasins you've made me."

"Get a move on, now. We've a ways to go before we get someplace where I can drop you."

"What do you mean? Aren't you taking me home?"

"No, I'm not. I'm getting myself back to headquarters, so to speak." James was pushing everything into their buckets.

"And where is that?"

"Best you don't know. After all, what do I know about you?"

Alex tried to look mysterious and dangerous. "I could be the runaway son of a rich English lord. Maybe that British ship was looking for me!"

"Yeah, I'll just bet you're royalty. With no clothes to speak of — not even boots!"

"Even princes have to go for a swim sometimes. I had clothes, but they blew away."

"Good job you found your breeches, at least," said James, breaking into loud guffaws.

Alex didn't think he needed to be that amused. And he wished he'd found his shirt, for it wasn't only his feet that were hurting. His chest and shoulders were scratched, too, and even bleeding. Some August mosquitoes had been taking bites out of his back.

James stopped guffawing and started talking again. "My father was a farmer too," he said. "I guess it wasn't too bad a deal for the rest of the family, but it wasn't the life for me — toiling in the fields from sunup till sundown."

"Yeah," said Alex. "I know what you mean. A pirate doesn't have to work so hard."

"Who said I was a pirate?"

"Well, you are, aren't you? Otherwise, why would you have all that gold? Did you rob that British ship?"

"Naw, we'd never rob anybody. Maybe we just took what was rightfully ours." James smiled. "Anyway, I've told you too much already. I know I'm a sucker for helping strays, but I'm not giving you our secrets. We've talked long enough. Now, let's get a move on."

◇

Early that afternoon, they came to a sunny spot with fewer trees and thick bushes. Alex's heart leapt for joy. Yes, he was right. It was a raspberry patch. James stopped at once and began pulling berries off the branches and throwing them into his mouth. Alex scrambled over to an even thicker patch of canes and joined the feast.

The berry canes were so heavy with fruit that when Alex shook a branch, a dozen fell into his outstretched hand. As he shovelled the plump, moist berries into his mouth, he began to feel much less thirsty and hungry. He and his companion ate silently. Small animals scampering in the underbrush and cicadas humming in the heat made the only sounds.

Then a strange feeling came over Alex. He thought he smelled something strong and dreadful. He looked up, chewing on his last handful of raspberries. Not more than fifty feet in front of him a huge black bear was nosing into the raspberry canes! The southwest breeze was carrying the bear's scent to them but not their scent to it. Alex froze to the spot.

"She hasn't seen us yet," James whispered. "Steady, boy."

The stifling smell of the bear was growing stronger and stronger. Alex had to put his hand over his mouth to keep from coughing.

"Now, move very slowly toward that tree over there." James pointed to the nearest maple tree. Alex wondered what good that would do. It was too high for him. But he didn't think this was the best time to argue.

Very slowly, James parted the canes and almost pushed his young friend in front of him. They inched along toward the tree.

They were almost to the tree when they heard a low, vicious growl.

"Run for it!" said James.

Alex was a fast runner and reached the tree first. He wasn't sure how it happened, but he felt James give him a push on his seat, and he was up that tree in no time. James was perched on a limb across from him.

Seconds later, the bear reached the tree.

Alex stared straight down at the animal, as the bear stood up on its hind legs and clawed at the tree. Could it uproot the tree? The bear seemed big enough to knock it right over. And the beast seemed to be growing in size as Alex glared down at it.

Then, in a horrific moment, the cold, beady eyes just above the black rubbery nose looked straight up at him.

The bear opened its mouth. It was a dark cavern with long, sharp teeth the size of stump pullers. Alex had told Ann that bear teeth were that large, but he didn't really believe it himself. He believed it now, though!

Alex was shaking like a leaf. Would he fall right into that mouth and be mangled to bits? He thought he could already hear the bear's teeth crunching.

"Steady, boy!" James said in a low voice. "She's not coming up here. Look down the trail."

Alex shifted his eyes without even moving his head and saw three baby cubs at the edge of the clearing. The mother bear knew they were there too, and turned her head.

Then — Bangg! Pfff! A musket shot whizzed past the wild animal.

Alex stopped shaking and went stiff. Was someone trying to kill him? or James?

"Be quiet!" James hissed from the opposite branch.

Three British sailors appeared at the edge of the clearing. They'd scared the bear back to her cubs, and were busy reloading.

"Now's our chance," said James. He dropped to the ground. "C'mon, Alex! We'll make a run for it!"

Alex shinnied down the tree, not even feeling the new scrapes and scratches on his legs as he slid past the rough bark.

James was back in the berry patch, grabbing their gear. "Quick, this way!" he said. "We'll be safe in that woods. They'll never follow us there!"

"What about the bear?" gasped Alex.

"They'll get her," said James.

"What about the cubs?" Alex said, looking back.

"Hey, boy, what about *us*!" James gave Alex a shove ahead. Alex almost fell forward, but James grabbed his hand. Together, they ran for the cover of the trees.

They could hear more musket shots behind them. Were they meant for the bear or for Alex and James? Alex wasn't going to wait around to find out. Maple saplings and Virginia creeper slashed against the boy's face and arms, but James did not stop, so Alex kept running, too.

They kept on for miles and miles, it seemed, and James steadily pushed ahead. "James!" Alex finally shouted after what seemed like hours. "I have to stop."

To his relief, James turned and came back. "I think we're out of their way now," James said quietly, leaning against a big pine tree, "so we can slow down some. We've come a good distance since yesterday. We'll soon be across this peninsula and bound to come out at Lake Ontario, not far from the place where we picked you up."

"But we'll still be across the lake from Hay Bay," said Alex. He was starting to get his bearings. "I don't know how we'll get across into the bay without a bateau, or even a canoe."

James grinned. "I'm a pirate, remember? If a farmer won't lend us a boat, we'll steal one."

Alex thought about this. "I'm not a pirate," he said firmly. "I don't steal boats, even if that means I have to take the long way around." Alex looked down at his swollen, aching feet and groaned.

James looked at the boy with something like respect.

CHAPTER
NINE

Alex awoke to the smell of fish sizzling in the pan over a smoky fire. He sat bolt upright. Above him, fresh-cut spruce boughs sent their lively aroma into the morning air. They formed the roof of the shelter that James had built the night before.

Alex listened to the sounds of warblers waking up in their spruce-tree homes. Then something dawned on him and he sprang out of the shelter and crossed over to the fire.

"Fish!" Alex shouted. "Fish!"

"Hey, not so loud! You'll wake more birds up!" James laughed, his moustache twitching and his eyebrows lifting.

"But if you have fish ... that must mean there's a *lake* nearby! We couldn't see it last night because it was dark, right? ... but ... how far is it?"

"Go see for yourself, then come back and help me eat. I caught this beauty at the crack of dawn and I'm hungry!"

Alex pulled on his moccasins and raced through the woods in the direction James had pointed. Along the way he began to catch glimpses of water between the trees. He burst out of the woods and stopped short. Right in front of him was a quiet, glassy lake, too small to be Lake Ontario. It must be where James had fished for breakfast. Alex marveled at the beautiful calm scene — a peaceful oasis in the middle of the wild forest.

"Keep going, and you'll see a sight!" he heard James call. So Alex went on. He had walked about one hundred yards down slightly sloping ground when he caught a glimpse of light and water through the trees ahead. He had just left the lake behind him, but here was water in front of him. Had he gotten turned around? Probably. But he was curious and so pushed between the thick grove of trees and came out to a grand sight. Here was *another* body of water. And this time he recognized it!

At his feet was a sheer drop, and at the foot of the cliff — Lake Ontario! They were almost home! Well, not quite, but from this high point, Alex could see for miles across the blue sparkling water of Lake Ontario and the green bushland on the other side. He recognized the familiar horizon of Adolphustown, the township that was beside his home township of Fredericksburgh. He'd often been down there with Father and Ryan and looked across Lake Ontario and up to the height where he now stood. He had wondered what it was like up there. Little did they know that Alex would be at that very spot one day, eating breakfast with a pirate!

Alex turned around and headed back to the smell of smoke. In a few minutes, he bounded through the trees and sat down on the ground beside the fire.

"We're almost home, aren't we, James!" he cried. He was juggling the hot piece of fried fish between his two hands, eager to bite into it.

"Yep. Pretty soon you'll be back with your kinfolk."

"And how about you? Where will you be?"

James looked down in silence. His lower jaw was set in a hard line. Alex suspected that James did not know what he would do next.

"Well, when I tell Father how you saved me, he won't turn you in, even if you are a pirate," said Alex. "He's really strict and even mean sometimes, but he's fair. I'd tell him the British sailors nearly caught you back there because you'd slowed down to rescue me!"

"Yes, if they'd caught me, I wouldn't have stood a chance," said James so lost in thought that he didn't see the grim look on Alex's face. "They always string up pirates first and ask questions later."

"Why are you a pirate then?"

A parade of puzzling expressions crossed James's face. "Well," he said, in a quiet tone, "I'm not sure myself, anymore. It was exciting for a while, but I'm getting tired of it. Maybe I'd like to go back home, too."

"Where's that?" Alex asked, reaching for another chunk of bass with his bare hands.

"No place in particular. You know, I may apply for one of those free land-grants that Upper Canada's new lieutenant-governor is offering to Americans just now. What's his name?"

"John Graves Simcoe."

"Yes, that's it. You know, I just might apply. I don't

have a criminal record as yet, so there's still a chance."

Alex spat out a mouthful of bones. "What about the gold?" he asked curiously.

James frowned. "You'd better forget about that, right quick. And if any of my buddies comes around asking about it, say you don't remember a thing. The less you know, the safer you'll be." He stared at Alex fiercely. "And don't be telling your pa, either. Swear, now."

"I swear I won't tell Father," said Alex quickly, before James remembered he had a brother, too.

"Now, let's go look at the lake again and figure out our journey from here."

Back at the edge of the woods, Alex gazed down at the lake and home.

"We could swim across," said Alex. He was tempted to try, at least.

"It's farther than it looks," warned James.

Alex sighed. Then he had another idea. "You have a hatchet. We can cut down a tree and hollow it out into a floating log. With two paddles, we can get across!"

"That part's right," said James. "But we've run out of food. We'll have to fish and hunt as we go. And it'll take a few days to make a reliable boat. Those waves can come up suddenly. We don't want to be taken by surprise out there!"

◇

"The stars are bright tonight," said James. "And just look at that full moon. I think she's smiling on us, my boy."

"I'm sure she is, James." Alex turned over on his spruce-bough bed and gazed up at the full moon.

Another day had passed and the unlikely pair had found their way down the steep hill to the shore of Lake Ontario. They'd caught only a bony sucker for supper, but were one step closer to Alex's homecoming. Alex could hardly wait, although he did get a knot in his stomach whenever he thought about facing his father.

"James?" said Alex.

No sound came from his friend.

"James," Alex repeated more loudly. This time he heard a low grunt.

"What do you want now?" James grumbled.

"Well, I just want you to know that it's been really exciting. And now that we're almost home, there's no need to rush. We could take our time. I'm not really looking forward to being chewed out by my father. And I kind of like this way of life."

"You *do*, do you!" James sounded irritated. "Well, I assure you that you are going to be home within the week — whether you like it or not!"

Alex grimaced. James was hard to understand some-times — just like all grown-ups. Here he was, giving the man a compliment, and James was practically insulting him in return! It was downright annoying!

◇

"Wake up, boy," growled a strange voice. Alex blinked and looked up a deerskin pantleg to the face of a frowning dark-skinned man.

His eyes shot wide open as he sat up and looked for James. His friend was gone and a low fire was smouldering. Then he knew where James was. He'd gone fishing for breakfast. That's why he'd started the fire. They had been in this same spot for a week now, and James had gone fishing every morning at this time.

"You spend your time sleeping, lazy boy?" said the man, shaking his head. "You should get up and feed the fire!"

Alex woke up really fast, then, and jumped over to the little pile of kindling and sticks that James had set there. He threw a few pieces onto the fire and tried to poke the few remaining embers to life with a long stick.

The man sat on a log on the other side of the fire. Alex and James had been carving it for the last three days, trying to make it into a boat to cross the lake. But it wasn't a boat yet. Alex was starting to wonder if it ever would be.

"Have you travelled far?" Alex asked the stranger in as friendly a tone as possible, although his voice shook slightly.

"Not far," said the man. His voice was softer now and he spoke with a slight accent. English was not his first language.

"Do you live near here?" Alex asked.

"Yes ... we did ... ten years ago," said the man.

"Ah," said Alex. He understood, now. The British had bought land from the Mississaugas along Lake Ontario — as far as a man could walk due north from the lake in one day. Some day, Alex would receive a portion of this land free of charge, for he was the son of a Loyalist. Alex got up and threw a bigger chunk of wood in the fire. Then he sat down and watched it closely to see if it would catch.

"Yes, we sold some land. Then we moved north," said the man, still staring into the fire.

Alex did not know if the man was happy about it or not. "Well, this is grand country," he said. "But I'll bet it's even grander up north where you live!"

Silence fell heavy between them.

This fellow was not friendly, Alex decided. He almost gasped as a thought hit him. Maybe there were even more unfriendly types about. Maybe James had been taken away while he, Alex, had slept. He'd heard of men captured with a hand over the mouth or one blow to the head. Yes, that's how it must have happened! He could feel chills tingling up his back.

Poor James! He was probably strung up on a tree somewhere. And here he was alone with a silent stranger who had called him lazy and had forced him to get up and feed the fire. Now what did he want a fire built up for? *To heat up irons for branding a boy?* If only Ryan knew the trouble he was in now — and so close to home, too!

Sweat was breaking out on Alex's forehead and starting to roll down his face. It was running into his eyes and dripping off his nose. He would have liked to move farther from the fire, but fear rooted him to the spot.

Then he started to shake. The man was staring at him with a gleam in his eye. Was he dreaming up some terrible torture?

Alex thought he heard the sound of feet approaching. He stared at his visitor by the fire, but saw no response. Then he looked up and saw two men, dressed like this one, coming along the pathway. This was going to end badly. He knew it. Three against one man and a boy would be too much — even for James.

He hung his head in despair and tried to gulp in extra air.

A light-hearted song floated out of the woods, and Alex jerked his head up again. There was James, just behind the men, whistling away like a warbler, with a whole line of suckers and a big pickerel slung over his shoulder.

"Alex, look at my catch!" Alex gaped at the two strangers more than the fish. "And meet my friends. I see you've already met Frank." James smiled at the man sitting on the half-made boat.

Alex stared at Frank, who broke into a wide smile. "Your boy decided to build up the fire. It had almost gone out when I got here."

"Good work, Alex!" said James. "Now, we'll have us some feed."

"And then we'll take you across the lake in our canoe," said Frank.

Alex sighed with relief and jumped up on wobbly legs to help James clean the fish. While he worked, he stole looks at Frank. Alex was feeling ashamed of himself for the way his imagination had run away with him. The man was a lot like Father, now he thought about it. He looked different, mind you — his hair was dark where Father's was red, and their eyes were different colours. But both men had the same sharp look to them. And, though Alex's father was a farmer and this man was a hunter, *they both liked to make boys work!*

CHAPTER
TEN

"It's not far now," said Alex, as they broke into a clearing he recognized. "Ryan and I pick berries here all the time."

"Then it's goodbye," said James, putting a hand on Alex's shoulder. "I'll just go far enough to see that your folks are still there."

"What do you mean, still there? Of course, they'll be there! Where else would they be?" Alex stared at James.

"They could be out looking for you. You've been gone for two weeks, lost in the bush — or even drowned, as far as they know."

"But I … " Alex was worried now. What if they'd really thought that? Then he shook his head. "Ryan will have set them straight," he declared. "He'll know I'm not drowned."

"If I were your father, I'd give you a good tanning," said James. "And I guess you deserve it."

"I do not! You *kidnapped* me, James."

"Well, no one made you get on our bateau. No one at all." James shook his head. "In fact, you begged us to take you aboard."

Alex stared at James. He had forgotten that part. Maybe this homecoming wasn't going to be so great after all. "You're coming with me, aren't you, James?"

"I have to move on. Your father wouldn't want to meet a pirate anyway."

"Well, I won't tell if you don't."

"Then how do you explain being gone?"

"I can't really. But Father is a fair man. You helped me when the others would have left me stranded. He'll help you for that reason."

"Well … "

"Besides, you have no food."

"Yeah, but I can hunt and fish. I won't starve."

"Where are you headed now?"

"Not sure!" James shifted the makeshift pack on his shoulder.

"When are you going back for the gold?" Alex stared up at him, eager for another adventure. "Why don't we tell Father about it? We'll get a great canoe and we could go back together."

"No, Alex. You promised you'd forget about that gold."

"All right, all right. But c'mon and meet the folks. It's not far … it's right through these trees."

"Well, I suppose," said James.

They walked on in silence with Alex leading the way. He couldn't believe he was almost home.

Half an hour later, Alex stepped out into his home clearing. He'd been gone only two weeks, but the corn had grown so much that it hid the clearing and the lower part of the cabin from view. Alex started to make his way between the rows of corn, twisting and turning to avoid the sharp-edged leaves. Then he stopped. He was eager to see Ryan, and some of Ann's baking would go down easily about now. But he wasn't so sure about Father. Maybe James was right. Under the circumstances, Alex thought, it might be a good idea to do some advance scouting.

So he backed out of the corn and made his way to his favourite climbing tree, motioning to James to stay back. Cautiously, he peered out between the leaves.

Alex's mouth fell open. What was going on? There was a huge crowd in the dooryard.

Everyone had heard of the tragedy — the drowning of the O'Carr twin. After a few days, almost everyone had given up hope of seeing the boy alive again. But the boy's twin, Ryan, had not. So the search had lasted for nearly two weeks. Now on this late August day the family was finally holding Alex's funeral. Rough-hewn benches had been placed in rows across the front yard, and the circuit-riding Methodist minister, the Rev. William Losee, had come to give the eulogy.

Neighbours and friends from as far away as Adolphustown and Appanea Falls had come to mourn with the family. Some stared straight ahead; others spoke to their neighbours in low tones.

"The boy thinks his brother is still alive," said one of the women sitting in the sunny meadow in front of the O'Carrs' cabin.

"Yes, a bit touched in the head he is, I reckon," said her husband, chewing on a piece of wild rye.

"Well, that's not unusual for a twin. The two had never been separated before, I hear. And the drowned one was the leader."

"Yep, with no leader, what happens to the follower? Goes a bit 'round the bend, I should think."

Ryan heard them as he crouched at the little window in his loft room, looking out over the crowd. *I know Alex is still alive*, he told himself. *I knew it the day he disappeared and I've known it ever since then.*

But even Father didn't believe him. Father had sent neighbours to Adolphustown, all the way to King's Town, and even across the whole of Prince Edward County — all looking for Alex. He'd asked Tówi and his other Mohawk friends, and young runners were sent through the woods. Swimmers had dived into Hay Bay again and again, searching for Alex's body, but only some of his clothes were found. His breeches had never shown up, mind you, but Father said they'd probably been washed far out into Lake Ontario with Alex's body.

A shadow fell across the room where Ryan was still kneeling at the window.

"We have to go down," said a voice. Ryan turned around, surprised out of his daydreams. It was Kate. Her eyes were red and swollen, and tears were streaming down her cheeks. She walked slowly over to the window beside Ryan and put both arms around him. He shivered a little under her touch, but did not move.

"We have to go down" she repeated.

"I can't," said Ryan. "They think Alex is drowned and I'm crazy! But they're the crazy ones. I won't go down."

"I know that you are not crazy, but they need to see that too. You have to come down."

"No!"

"Ryan … "

Father poked his head in the doorway. "This is sad enough without you making things worse. You go on, and I'll attend to Ryan."

"No, I will not go! I'm staying here with Ryan until he's ready to go down!" Kate squeezed her lips tighter together and put her hands on her hips. Her eyes were flashing. "Albert!" she called.

Albert stepped out of Kate's old bedroom. "Yes?"

"Father doesn't want me to stay with Ryan. Will you please see if you can talk some sense into him?"

"What's happening up there?" Ann shouted from the foot of the ladder leading to the loft. "The minister is calling for the mourners now."

Kate stood her ground. Father grabbed her arm in silence. Albert stepped forward. Then suddenly, Ryan rose from his spot at the window and stepped beside Kate. "I'm ready to go now. This isn't real, anyway, so it doesn't matter." Father dropped Kate's arm as young Ryan led the way to the ladder.

So the mourners filed down onto the main floor of the cabin and then out the front door, Ryan showing no sign of emotion, Kate following in tears, Albert walking beside her with his arm around her shoulders. The solemn-faced David O'Carr walked along beside his wife, who was dabbing her eyes with a lace-edged handkerchief.

The family filed into the front row. Ryan slumped down on the bench as far away from the others as he could. Flies hummed and bees buzzed among the wild carrot blossoms at the edge of the cornfield. A goldfinch flew past the makeshift tree-stump pulpit.

"We are gathered here today," the minister announced, "to remember a fine young man, Alexander Berton O'Carr, known to us as Alex. The tragic circumstances surrounding his death have not been made clear to us at this time, but we do know that the Almighty looks down upon us this day and knows the reason for such tragedy and sadness, though we may never know."

A sigh rippled across the gathering. An old lady coughed and a baby gurgled. Cicadas droned in the distance.

"Alex was well liked by all who knew him," the minister continued. "He was a lively, energetic young man, who accepted life bravely for his tender years. He faced all adversity and hardship with courage. He worked with great diligence, never neglecting his duties as a son and as a brother."

That sounded like an exaggeration to Ryan. Did no one tell the minister what Alex was doing the day he disappeared?

"He was the most dutiful of all sons," the preacher went on, "the most honest of all children, the most energetic of all workers …"

Ryan snorted, then quickly looked down at Baron, who was snoring quietly at his feet. His brother was certainly not the bravest and most energetic of all. So why was the Reverend going on so much? It was too bad Alex couldn't hear this. For Ryan himself, a lot of praise was embarrassing, but Alex just lapped it up!

Then a strange feeling came over Ryan. He felt as if Alex was already listening to the minister and was not far away. Ryan stared toward the woods. There was no sign of anyone. Maybe he was touched in the head, just as the neighbours said.

"Hoo-hu-wooo!" Ryan sat bolt upright, and Baron woke up with a snort, stood up, and made a mad dash for the woods.

The bees kept buzzing in the late-afternoon sun and the minister kept reading from Psalm 23: "Yea, though I walk through the valley of the shadow of death, I will fear no evil …" From his bench, Ryan thought he heard a rustling in the corn patch and turned around to look. Was it Baron, chasing a skunk through the field? He was barking now, loud enough to wake the dead.

"… Thou preparest a table before me in the presence of mine enemies.… "

"Hoo-hu-woo!"

That did it. Ryan leapt up from the bench and charged over to the cornfield. It wasn't Baron making all the commotion; it was …

"Alex!"

A tanned and dirt-stained boy tumbled out from behind the moving cornstalk and hugged Ryan as tightly as a bear.

"Alex! I knew it was you! I knew you were alive!"

"Yeah … I'm home!"

The minister clamped his Bible shut and opened his mouth in shock. "Well, I ... " He turned to the boys' father and sister. "Is this ... is ...?"

Father and Kate couldn't hear him. They were racing over to the patch of grass beside the cornfield where the twins were giggling and punching each other, and Baron was running round and round in circles, barking with joy.

"I've been with ... " Alex tried to explain. "Well, meet my friend James." Alex turned and everyone looked behind Alex, but no one was there. "James!" Alex shouted. "James!"

The whole crowd of mourners had clustered around to look at the walking miracle.

"We thought you'd drowned," said Father. "We are having a funeral."

"Yeah, I heard," Alex said, grinning. It had really been something, hearing all those great things said about him.

"You have no idea," said Kate, still crying — but from shock, not grief. "These past two weeks ... How could you *do* this to us?"

"I ... I ... well." Alex looked up at the whole crowd of neighbours, friends, and relatives staring at him in silence.

"I ... "

"Well, never you mind. You're back, you're alive, and that's all that matters," Kate said more calmly. "We thought we'd never see you again this side of heaven."

By now the minister had come to his senses. He took his place at the front again. "This *is* a happy day!" he cried.

"The lost is found. God moves in a mysterious way His wonders to perform." In a wavering voice, he began to sing a hymn.

> *O for a thousand tongues to sing*
> *My great Redeemer's praise,*
> *The glories of my God and King,*
> *The triumphs of His grace.*

Everyone scrambled back to their benches and the thunderous sound of singing voices reached the tree-tops. Alex moved in beside Ryan on the front bench and started belting out the words. He wouldn't have missed this for the world! After all, how many people get to sing at their own funeral!

PART THREE

Ryan's Storm

CHAPTER
ELEVEN

Ryan woke up and peered over the side of the feather bed. Alex was still asleep beside him and the house was as quiet as a forest clearing. Outside the window, Ryan could see snowflakes falling down thickly.

Six months had passed since Ryan's twin had reappeared in the corn patch right in the middle of his own funeral. That hot August afternoon seemed like a dream now — the bees buzzing, the cornstalks moving in the breeze, and Alex bursting in on the scene. For weeks afterwards, Alex had been the hero of the township. Of course, he basked in the glory of it. All fall and all winter, he'd been telling the story of his adventure, and he kept adding more parts as time passed.

Ryan soon got tired of his brother's bragging. He was also getting tired of the way the neighbours kept thinking he was a bit touched in the head. Somehow, they'd forgotten that Ryan had been right all along, that Alex was still alive.

Why does Alex get all the praise around here? Ryan thought. *He may be brave, but I think I was brave, too — waiting all that time for him to come home.*

Ryan turned over for a few more minutes of sleep. After all, it was February and there was no reason to get out of bed soon. There wasn't much farm work to do, and in the winter, the snow was too deep to travel to Appanea Falls for school. It was a good thing Ryan and Alex could read, write, and do some arithmetic already. That was thanks to Ann and Kate.

"Kate!" Ryan said out loud and jumped out of bed. He'd just remembered. Kate and Albert were coming today!

Ryan raced over to the chair where he'd left his clothes the night before. He pulled on his woollen underwear and his long wool stockings and breeches. They were so cold, that he wished he'd warmed them under the quilts during the night.

With his right hand, he combed back the shock of thick blond hair that had fallen across his forehead. Still in his sock feet, he padded across the room and opened the door into the small hallway. The heat rising through the opening in the hall floor felt great, but not as inviting as the strong smell of frying pork and hot toast.

As Ryan climbed down the ladder, the hot air coming from the roaring fire in the kitchen fireplace welcomed him.

"Morning, Ryan," said Ann. She filled a bowl with oatmeal porridge and set it down on the table. "Guess you're up early because Kate's coming."

"Yes!" said Ryan, grinning.

Thump, thump! It was Alex jumping down from the ladder.

"I didn't know you were awake, Alex," said Ryan.

"Kate's coming!" said Alex. "I have to be awake!"

"I'll have some more toast," said Father, scooping out two heaping spoonfuls of strawberry jam onto his plate.

Ann went over to the fireplace, put two thick pieces of bread in a toast holder, and held it above the fire. After flipping them, she gave them a few minutes more. She moved slowly now because she was soon going to have a baby. She handed the slices to her husband.

"Albert and I will be home before dark," said Father. "Are you sure you'll be all right?"

Father was going to check his trapline with Albert while Kate stayed at the house to visit all day. Tomorrow, Kate and Albert would start back to their temporary home — the Shaws' shanty. Kate had been given her lot in Fredericksburgh Township, on the other side of the Original Road. So Albert had traded his lot to the south for the one beside Kate's, to ensure that they would have a good-sized farm. Kate and Albert had spent the summer clearing as much as they could. Then, as soon as the cold weather arrived, they had moved in with the Shaws for the winter.

Ryan was planning to coax his sister to stay over a couple of days. He'd persuade her to correct some of his exercises in arithmetic and reading. She couldn't resist helping him with his studies.

"I'm fine, David," said Ann. "Our little one isn't due for a full three weeks yet. And I'll have Kate and the boys with me." She smiled at Alex and Ryan, but Ryan noticed for the first time that Ann looked worried.

Rap, rap, bang. Bang, rap, bang.

It was Albert, thumping on the front door. Ryan could tell. He had hands as big as a bear's paws.

Alex and Ryan raced to open the door, but Alex got there first. He slipped the bolt and opened the door wide. In tumbled Bobcat! Albert and Kate came in right behind, all wrapped up in raccoon coats and layers of scarves and woollen mitts.

"Well, here we are, safe and sound, and we didn't even flip the flat sleigh once!"

"Kate!" Alex and Ryan buried their faces in her snow-covered coat.

"Hello, boys! Glad to see me?" Kate's eyes under her scarves were bright and merry. "You'll never guess what I've brought you!"

"Candy!" shouted Alex.

"Some paper?" guessed Ryan hopefully. That would fit right in with his plans.

"Neither!" said Kate, and moved aside. Right in front of Albert was another ball of raccoon fur. There was a long, green scarf and white-blond hair on top of it, sticking out from under a red woollen toque. It was Albert's young brother, Geordie.

"What's he doing here?" Ryan asked.

Kate explained while helping Geordie off with his clothes. "Betsy and Nancy tease him all day long, and his baby sister needs a lot of attention. So he wishes every day of his life that he had big brothers like you two. He was really excited about coming to visit."

"Where's Sarah?"

"She's too busy filling her hope chest. She's marrying Daniel in May."

The boys remembered how busy Kate had been while she was preparing for her wedding. Then Ryan said, "He has Albert."

"Bertie doesn't have any time to play with him. He's as busy as his Pa."

"Well, he gets to see you all the time, and we don't. That's not fair!" said Alex.

Geordie strutted over to the fireplace to warm himself. Kate looked from one twin to the other. She didn't say anything, but she looked disappointed.

"Well, I suppose, we could think about it … playing with him, that is." Ryan knew there wasn't any way out of it, so they might as well resign themselves.

"We could take him out to the shanty to see Baron," said Alex, not to be outdone.

"That's my boys," said Kate, smiling broadly.

Geordie had been following this with a smirk on his face. As soon as Kate's back was turned, Alex stuck his tongue out at the boy.

"When you get warm, come over and have some johnny cake," Ann said.

Geordie marched right over and took two pieces — one in each hand. The boys stared. Kate would have yelled at them if they'd been that greedy at his age.

"Come, Alex and Ryan. That means you, too," said Ann. "There's plenty of johnny cake for everyone."

Alex followed Ryan over to the table, where Geordie now sat beside the cake. They eyed him suspiciously.

"Have you got our food pack ready, Ann?" said Father.

"Right here," said Ann. The twins stared at the huge pack of food that Ann handed to each of them.

"That ought to last for a week," said Alex. "Did you leave anything for us?"

"Never fear," said Ann. "There's plenty in the cold cellar to last for a year."

"They can't forget," said Kate quietly. She put an arm around her brothers, who were sitting on each side of her now.

"Well, I don't intend to be gone a week, but it's always wise to take extra — just in case. Now, I think we should be off, Albert."

Father took his raccoon coat off the hook and threw it around his shoulders. Then he came back and gave Ann a quick kiss. "We'll be back by dark," he said.

"No need to hurry," said Ann. "I have plenty of help here."

"Why can't I go out trapping with you, Albert?" whined Geordie. Ryan could see that he was putting on a baby act to get his own way. He hoped it would work.

"Not this time," said Albert, standing at the open door. "The snow's too deep out there. You couldn't get through because your legs aren't long enough."

Geordie made a face and climbed up into a big chair by the fireplace. Father and Albert sat down on the bench by the front door of the kitchen and tied their flat, webbed snowshoes to their boots. Father had built a fine parlour for Ann, but in winter, they didn't use it at all. No one had time to keep a fire going in the parlour *and* the kitchen.

Ryan looked out the front window as Father and Albert tramped toward the woods, keeping their feet wide apart so they wouldn't trip on their snowshoes. Baron bounded along behind them for a few feet, then gave up and came back to the front door. Ryan felt happy he wasn't out in all that snow. This was his seventh winter in Canada, and he had decided that he was a summer person.

"Ouch!" yelled Geordie over by the fireplace. Alex was standing a few inches from Geordie, laughing and looking sneaky.

"He punched me in the arm," said Geordie, pointing to Alex.

"I was only teasing," said Alex. "Can't he take a joke?"

"Alex, that's no way to behave," said Kate. "Now, Ann, what shall we do first?"

"The washing," said Ann, and Ryan groaned. That job was sure to keep Kate busy all day long. Some visit!

Alex glared at Ann. "I don't know why you have to wash when Kate's here."

"I'm sorry, boys, but I haven't had the time … "

"You don't have to apologize, Ann," said Kate, standing beside her stepmother with her hands on her hips. "We have to get everything ready for the new arrival and that includes doing the wash. The boys are old enough to understand that."

Ryan and Alex looked at each other. Whose side was Kate on, anyway?

Kate saw their look, and hurried over to give them each a hug. "Take Geordie outside and play in the snow for a while," she said quietly. "Then this afternoon, I'll spend all my time with my two brothers."

Ryan brightened. When Kate spoke that firmly, they knew her mind was made up and nothing would change it. "Well, Alex," he said, slapping his brother on the shoulder, "Geordie can help us make our slide!"

Kate smiled and patted Ryan on the shoulder. Alex glared at him.

Geordie's eyes looked even bigger in his small face as Kate helped him put on his raccoon coat. Then she pushed the red woollen toque onto his head and wound his green scarf around his neck and head, as Geordie pulled on his red mitts. Ryan and Alex dressed themselves: Ryan in his red woollen coat and scarf, and Alex in blue.

"Now, don't go far," said Ann, "and stay away from the bay. That little stream by the woods will make a great slide."

"We'll be fine, Ann," said Alex. He was getting over his angry spell. Kate patted him on the shoulder too. "And no more brave adventures for you, young man," she said.

Alex was beaming now. Kate sure knew the right thing to say to get Alex on her side. But Ryan was sick of hearing about his brave twin! It had been a terrible time for the family, and if Alex had obeyed Father, he wouldn't have got into trouble in the first place.

Ryan pushed on outside ahead of Alex and Geordie. The sun was out bright and full and the snow was almost blinding. The air was strangely warm, too. "Hey, we may get a spring thaw," he said. "And then we'll have packing snow. We could make a snowman or a fort!"

"Naw!" said Alex. "It would just melt in that sun." He hurried on toward the woods while Ryan and Geordie followed. They walked briskly along their usual woodland trail, the sun shining brightly and a new, warmish breeze rippling across the snow. It was a great day to be outside.

"Why can't we slide there?" asked Geordie, pointing ahead through the leafless maple trees to the sparkling ice. "It doesn't look far."

"Good idea!" said Alex, smiling at Geordie. Maybe the kid wasn't so bad, after all. "I'll bet the sliding's good there. The wind blows the snow off the bay. It makes great clear patches."

"No," said Ryan. "Ann told us to stay away from the bay. Besides, you know yourself that bay ice is too dangerous."

Alex stopped under a big spruce. "What's Ann got to do with it?" he yelled. "You're just a spoil-sport!" A clump of snow dropped down beside him from a branch above.

"Look at that snow, Alex! It's melting. The ice could start melting, too. And that won't be safe! Besides, we shouldn't worry Ann just now."

Another pile of snow crashed to the ground, barely missing Alex's head. "What she doesn't know won't hurt her," he said.

Ryan moved closer to Alex. "Geordie would tell."

"He's the one who suggested it. He'd be telling on himself."

"You know *we'd* get the blame. We're older."

"Oh, come on, Ryan, don't be a coward!"

Ryan was getting mad now, madder than he'd ever been. "I'm not a coward! I just don't want to get blamed when it's not my fault — and I don't want to upset Ann."

"Ann, Ann, Ann! You're getting soft on me, Ryan. Next you'll be calling her 'Mother'!" Alex glared at his brother. "We're always upsetting her. What difference does it make?"

"She's soon going to have a baby! It's not good for her to get upset right now!"

"Did you say *baby*?" asked Geordie. He grabbed the back of Ryan's red scarf which was streaming out behind him. "Kate said it was some kind of *bird*!"

The twins exchanged startled glances, the tension broken.

"A stork?" asked Alex. "Was she talking about a stork bringing us a baby?"

"Yes! But I thought it would bring a baby bird!"

Ryan and Alex howled with laughter. They laughed so hard they bent over and tears ran down their cheeks.

Geordie stared at the twins in silence and then his face grew red. He stomped on toward the bay, leaving them behind him.

"Oh, c'mon back, Geordie," Ryan yelled.

Geordie broke into a fast run, his bright green scarf flapping against his back.

CHAPTER
TWELVE

Geordie was small for a six-year-old, but he could run like a rabbit. Before the twins knew it, he'd reached the end of the trees and was headed right for the bay. Then he ran at top speed to the top of the sharp hill overlooking the bay. He sat down on the snow and slid in one great swoop right out onto the ice. Then he scrambled to his feet and was soon zigzagging across the hard surface.

"Geordie! Geordie!" the boys yelled, racing down the hill. "Come back, Geordie!"

Ryan hoped Geordie would hit a slippery patch and fall down, so they could catch up to him. But he didn't. Instead, Alex hit an ice patch and went sailing along on his seat till he came to a full stop. Then he just sat there yelling, "Come back!"

Ryan knew it was up to him. Alex was far behind now. He ran straight for Geordie, sliding over the slippery patches as best he could. He was gaining on Geordie.

Finally, Geordie hit an ice patch, fell down, and slid ahead on his seat. *Now, I'll catch him,* Ryan thought.

But he didn't see the dark blue patch of ice water just ahead of Geordie.

Neither did Geordie. The bright sun was blinding him. Too late, he saw the danger. He stopped at the very edge of the dark hole and turned away as quickly as he could, but fell on his stomach.

"Aaaaah!" His scream echoed across the ice.

Ryan watched in horror as Geordie slid slowly into the dark, cold water, feet first, his hands clutching at the icy edge of the hole. He could not save himself. First his feet, then his legs, then his waist and chest went under. Then only his arms and head were showing. Geordie clung to the snowy edge, too cold and shocked to yell anymore. But still he hung on.

For a moment, Ryan stared at Geordie's stricken face, unable to move. Then he clicked into action. "Hang on, Geordie!" he yelled, running toward the water. He hit the ice and slid forward slowly on his stomach, facing Geordie.

"Hang on! I'll get you," Ryan said. "Be very still."

Geordie didn't say a word, but his teeth were chattering. Ryan knew the child's whole body would soon be shaking with the cold. Then he would lose his hold.

"God help me," Ryan prayed. "Save us." His own teeth were chattering and he was shaking too. But he edged closer and closer. When he was a few feet from the shivering boy, he took off his coat and threw one end of it over the edge of the ice.

Geordie reached for the coat, but he couldn't touch it. So Ryan slid farther along the ice, praying he wouldn't go sliding right into Geordie.

It was then he felt the icy water rolling the ice under him like a wave. "Please, God," he breathed aloud. "Help!"

He inched farther along until finally the coat was within Geordie's reach. "One hand at a time, Geordie," he said. "Grab it one hand at a time."

Geordie grabbed the coat with one hand, but didn't want to let go of the side of the ice.

"Grab hold with the other hand, too. I'll pull you in," said Ryan.

At last Geordie grabbed the other side of the coat. Then Ryan started to pull his coat slowly, and inch by inch, toward the shore. But Geordie did not come up over the ice. The ice broke in front of him as he came forward.

Ryan could see that this wasn't going to work, but still kept pulling and backing up toward the shore. The nearer he got Geordie to shore, the safer it would be. Ryan knew he would never be able to swim in this cold. But if he could touch the lake bottom under the ice hole, then he would jump in and get Geordie out.

Just then, Alex yelled, "Here, Ryan. A log!"

"Hang on, Geordie," said Ryan. He didn't want to take his eyes off the child. But he had to turn around to look for the log. It skidded out toward him, stopping just out of his reach.

He turned back to Geordie. "Now, you keep hold of my coat!" he said. "We're getting closer to shore. The water will be shallow soon. Then I'll jump in and get you."

"Promise?" Geordie choked.

"I promise," said Ryan, trying to sound braver than he

felt. He hoped he could do it.

So Ryan kept pulling and pulling, and the ice kept cracking and cracking. Ryan could see Geordie was growing weaker. His face was completely white, and Ryan knew that if the child fell in, he was gone. He would not be able to find Geordie under the ice.

Just then, Geordie let go of the coat with his left hand.

Ryan lunged through the space between them and plunged into the freezing water.

He gasped with the icy cold but grabbed the drowning boy's hand. His fingers tightened around Geordie's.

Ryan's breath was coming short and fast. But his feet hit bottom. He wrapped both arms around Geordie and held him tightly.

Then, looking up, he saw the log pushing its way across the ice. Alex was at the other end of it.

"C'mon, Geordie. We can bottom it here," he said. Although the water was only to his waist, he was growing too cold and stiff to lift the little boy. Alex slid on his stomach with the log beside him. Then he grabbed Geordie's arms and pulled. Ryan pushed.

They pushed and pulled him right up onto the snowy shore. Then Alex held a hand out to Ryan and jerked him up and out of the icy water.

Alex whipped off his coat and wrapped it around Geordie. Then he tucked his arms under Geordie's head and shoulders while Ryan took his feet. Ryan was shaking so badly now that he could hardly keep up to his brother.

Alex began running. At first, Ryan felt he couldn't

keep going. He was shaking with cold, and his feet felt so heavy that he could barely lift them. His clothes were stiff with ice. But Alex kept running and pulling them both. Ryan ploughed along behind in a frantic daze.

Minutes later they reached the cabin.

"Help," yelled Alex. The door flew open. Kate stared at them in horror.

Ann's hands dropped from the petticoat she was scrubbing and rushed over to the boys. "Shut that door, Alex!" she said.

Ryan fell onto the floor beside Geordie. "They fell in the bay, Kate!" Alex was shouting. "Geordie fell into the bay! We pulled him out."

Kate grabbed Geordie and started pulling off his clothes. Ann took charge of Ryan, dragging him close to the fireplace and stripping off every stitch of his clothing. He would have been embarrassed if he wasn't so desperately cold.

Kate stripped Geordie and tapped his arms and legs. "He's not frozen," she said, "but he could catch his death of cold." Geordie's eyes were open now, and he was shaking all over. Ann set down her armload of quilts, grabbed Geordie, and plonked him into her washtub right on top of her pink petticoat.

"Kate," she said, "pour some hot water into that other tub. Ryan, come quick and get into this rinse tub." Ryan didn't need a second invitation. He came over and climbed in.

"How providential that we were washing today," said Ann with satisfaction. "This warm water is just the thing!"

There it is again, thought Ryan. *Ann thinks wash water solves all problems.* He began to laugh. *This time,* he thought, *she's right!*

———————◇———————

CHAPTER
THIRTEEN

"Are you all right, Ryan?" Ann asked.

"I'm fine," said Ryan. He was enjoying the mug of ginger tea his stepmother had made him "to heat up his insides." It had plenty of sugar, and the spicy flavour had warmed him up, just as Ann had predicted. But Geordie, tucked in next to him under the quilts and still shivering, had barely touched his.

"Come on, now, Geordie, drink up." Kate lifted the mug to the little boy's lips, but instead of sipping, he began to cry. "I was so scared," he said, "but Ryan came and got me."

Alex turned around on his chair beside the fireplace. "And I got the both of them. I had to pull them both home! So I guess that makes me a hero again."

"No!" said Geordie. "Ryan's the hero!"

"Well, you're all safe now," said Ann. "So it doesn't matter who got you. Here's a fresh mug of tea. I'm sure that one's gone stone cold."

"I don't want it!" grumbled Geordie. "I hate ginger tea."

"Please try a little," said Kate. She sighed and held the

cup to Geordie's lips. He took one sip. "Come, come, Geordie," she coaxed, "you have to take more."

Ryan swallowed the last of his tea, and felt completely restored. "I'm getting out of this dumb bed," he said. "I sure don't wanna stay here forever."

"Are you sure you're warm enough?" asked Kate, handing him dry clothes. Then she put her hand on Geordie's forehead and shook her head. She reached under the bed clothes and pulled out the heavy iron. "Give this to Ann to heat up, and bring me a hot one, would you? Geordie's feet are still ice-cold."

Ryan went back to the kitchen. Ann was bending over holding her stomach, and seemed to be holding her breath. She dropped her hands to her sides and stood up straight when Ryan came in.

"Is it the baby?" Ryan asked.

"No," said Ann. "It can't be. The baby's not due for three weeks yet. I'm just tired." She walked over to the fireplace and sat down in Father's big chair.

Kate stepped back into the kitchen, smoothing out her apron with her hands. "I'll finish the washing, Ann, and Ryan and Alex will help."

"Me?!" Alex yelled. "I don't know anything about washing!"

"I'll teach you," Kate said, pursing her lips.

"Ohhhh." A low moan came from Ann. She was rocking a little in the big chair that did not rock. Then she turned to face the fire. Kate and the twins looked at one another in alarm. They stood still and stared at her back.

A few minutes passed in silence. Then Kate set a

board in the washtub and said, "Now, boys, watch me."
She began to scrub a pair of breeches, rubbing them up
and down against the washboard. "Watch how I scrub
those dirty knees, where someone spilled bacon grease."

"You're doing fine, Kate," said Alex. "Keep going." He
smiled slyly at his brother.

Ryan didn't notice. He was listening to the wind. The
cabin had suddenly grown darker, though it was only
noon. A storm must be coming!

"Ryan." Kate's voice sounded scared. "Ryan, put all our
water in the big pans and hang them over the fire to
boil. Alex, fill all the empty pails with snow and bring
them in to melt."

"But, Kate," said Alex. "We don't need any more wash
water. We have enough."

"Just do it, Alex," said Kate. Something in her voice
filled the boys with alarm. Kate pointed to Ann. She was
rocking again, and holding her middle. "It's the baby,"
Kate whispered. "It's on its way. I don't know anything
about birthing babies, but I know we need to boil water."

Ryan stared at his sister. Kate had gone white and was
starting to tremble. "What's wrong, Kate?" asked Alex.

"Mother ... she died when you were born," Kate whispered to the boys. "She died so fast ... right after ... "
She sat down suddenly on the nearest chair and
dropped her head in her hands. "We need Mrs. Davis!
She's a good midwife. Father said so. Oh, if only Bertie
were here ... "

The kitchen was growing darker. Alex went to the
door and took a peek outside. "A storm's blowing in," he

whispered. "It looks too bad to go for Mrs. Davis. In this weather, you could get lost and have to hole up in the woods till morning."

"Ann won't have the baby right away, will she?" asked Ryan. "Father and Albert will be home soon. They'll know what to do."

"I hope so," sighed Kate, raising her head slightly.

"Are you getting that water on to boil?" asked Ann. She was sitting with her back to them. There was a new sharpness in her tone.

"Yes, Ann," said Kate. She hurried over to the fireplace with a bucket of water. She poured it slowly into the big kettle that nearly always boiled there. When she turned around to get the next bucket, she almost bumped into Ryan. He handed her the bucket, but was staring at Ann.

The firelight was dancing across his stepmother's face as she sat in front of the fire. Her lips were set in a tight line and her brows were drawn together. From time to time, the muscles in her face tightened even more. Ryan knew he had to go for help. He had to do it for Kate, and he had to do it for Ann. He respected Ann, he realized now, and was sorry for being so nasty to her. But he'd make it up to Ann. He'd go for Mrs. Davis.

"Now, boys, get snow into these tubs," Kate mumbled. She wrung out the last piece of clothing and handed Alex a tub. He threw on his coat and toque and hurried outside to scoop up snow. Ryan took the time to dress warmly. He put on his heavy raccoon coat and, over his toque, a long red wool scarf which he wound round and round his head. He put on extra socks and pulled on his boots.

"Well, you sure are taking your time for a trip just round the corner," said Ann impatiently. "Hurry up, Ryan."

He grabbed two pairs of mitts — his and Alex's — and headed for the door.

In the yard, he helped Alex finish scooping snow into the tub. A strong wind was starting to howl around the cabin.

"I'm going for Mrs. Davis," said Ryan.

Alex stared at his brother in shocked silence. "I don't think you should. Ann says the baby won't come yet. And I'm sure Kate can figure out what to do!"

"Kate's in no shape to deliver a baby. She still remembers our mother dying."

"But if you go, Kate and Ann will only worry, and that will make things worse! I don't think you should go, Ryan." Alex looked really worried now.

"I've got an idea, Alex. I think you can help."

"Doing what? I don't want to face that storm."

"You put a pillow on our bed and hump it all up. Tell Kate I felt chilled and I've gone up to the attic to bed. If she looks, she'll see the pillow and think I'm asleep."

"How can I do that? They'll know if you don't come back inside." Alex thought Ryan was going crazy from the cold.

"Kate's going to have to take Geordie out of that bedroom," Ryan said, "and put him back in the kitchen—and soon—to make room for Ann in her own bed. You can tell her I came in while she was in the bedroom with Geordie."

"But what if it doesn't work out like that?"

"Well, try something else, then. If you have to, tell her the truth. If things get bad, it may reassure her to know that help is on the way."

Together, they dragged the full tub of snow to the door. Then they stood up — face to face.

"Be careful, Ryan," said Alex. He took out a piece of cheese he'd kept in his pocket since breakfast. It was wet around the edges, but it was a big piece. "Here, take this," he said.

"Thanks," Ryan said. Then he stepped down off the stoop and headed for the old shanty. An extra pair of snowshoes was stored there.

Alex stood by the tub until Ryan came out of the shanty. He was still watching as Ryan set off to the southeast toward the Original Road.

CHAPTER
FOURTEEN

At first, the wind was blowing in from the northwest and slashing Ryan in the back. Then it swirled around to the west and started hitting his right side. He pulled his toque down over his forehead and pushed his red scarf up over his chin and nose. With all the extra wool covering his face and the gusts of snow circling him, he could barely see where he was going. But he knew the way, so he decided to trudge on, slow and steady. There would be no use rushing ahead blindly.

All around him the cedars and spruce stood green and silent, already part-covered in snow from the sudden storm. He just needed to get to the stream at the south edge of the farm. If he could cross over there, he would soon be on the Original Road. Ryan knew he had to be careful to keep going in the right direction. With no sun to guide him, he would have to rely on other things. There was a notch in a spruce ahead of him to the right. He and Alex and Father had cut those markers one warm week in October when the maples were red. How could this frozen, snow-covered place be the same forest?

As Ryan snowshoed past a clump of cedars, he came to a clearing and discovered he was already at the stream. He put one foot out on the ice. It seemed solid enough. Then he drew back. That snow could be covering a soft place. If the bay had open spaces, the stream would have more. It was constantly flowing, and that stopped it from freezing completely.

Well, I won't drown, thought Ryan. *It's too shallow for that.* But then he remembered what would happen if his feet got wet. He'd have to keep walking as they iced up. His feet could freeze and he could die from the frostbite. No, he couldn't risk that! He'd have to take the long way round to the Davises' farm.

Or did he? There was another shortcut, through the maple bush and over the Fletchers' farm. It would get him onto the Original Road less than a mile from the Davises'. But he had never gone that way alone.

Ryan hesitated for a moment. *If I get lost,* he thought, *no one will find me.* Even the crows and bluejays had found shelter and were waiting for the storm to end.

Then Ryan remembered Ann, groaning beside the fireplace, and the pain on her face, and he knew he had to go on. He plunged ahead, remembering all the good things Ann had done for him and Alex. She'd baked bread as good as any Kate had ever made — actually better, most of the time — and cookies and pies as well. She'd mended their clothes, and she hardly ever lost her temper the way Father often did.

She'd been the granddaughter of a real lord and she'd come to live in this lonely place. She'd played checkers with them and made up games. She'd even bought books in King's Town for Ryan to read — and a few for Alex, too. Ryan remembered he'd only given her a mumbly thank you for that, and he'd never really thanked Ann for much else.

Thank you, Ann, he said to himself, hoping God would send her the message. Then if she died before he got back, she would know he was sorry.

Then Ryan started wondering. Where was God, and why didn't He stop the snowstorm? For that matter, why had God sent the storm on the very day Ann was going to have her baby?

"Stop the storm, God!" Ryan yelled into the branches of the trees. "I've got to get to the Davises'!"

It was hard going, now. A thick grove of spruce and cedar blocked the sky out. But this was a good sign. Just beyond it lay the maple bush at the east end of their farm. They were going to tap it next spring and sell the maple syrup in King's Town. Ann had said that Alex and Ryan should be paid for helping tap the trees and make the syrup. Father would never have said such a thing.

As Ryan stepped into the open bush beyond the cedars, he looked up and saw a crow perched on a maple tree a few feet ahead of him.

What are you doing out here? thought Ryan. Tówi had once told him that crows were very intelligent. "I never can figure out why you settlers talk about wise old owls," said the Mohawk hunter. "Crows are much more clever, by far." But maybe even crows could get lost.

"Show me the way to the Davises'!" Ryan called.

"Caw, caw, caw!" the crow answered.

"That's no help!" Ryan shouted back. Then the crow lifted off and flew out of sight.

Ryan ploughed on through the maple bush.

It should be much brighter and easier to see things here, thought Ryan. *But it's not. It's just as dark as the cedar grove!* He pulled his scarf up a bit so he could see better. No wonder it was so dark. The storm was getting worse! A heavy white mist surrounded the maple trees, and large flakes of snow were tumbling down and sticking to the branches, the trunks, and Ryan's raccoon coat.

Ryan was still weak from the near-drowning that morning. His hands and arms were shaking, and he was getting hungry. He wondered if he'd end up eating tree bark before he got out of the woods.

Then he remembered the cheese Alex had given him. There it was, still in his pocket. He turned his back to the wind and ate it in great gulps. He ploughed on.

◇

Ryan knew it must have been an hour or more since he'd left the woods. Patches of trees and huge stumps were scattered in front of him, but there was no clear trail. Was he on the Original Road or was he still on the Fletchers' farm? It was impossible to tell. The trees and clear spots zigzagged ahead of him as far as he could see.

The snow kept hurtling down and the trees stood silently taking it all.

"Don't just stand there!" Ryan shouted angrily. "This is

an emergency!" If only the trees could talk and show him the way. They swayed and some of them creaked in the wind, but they gave Ryan no clues.

Ryan tried to move on, but he was exhausted. He sat down on one of the stumps to figure out his next move. He was so tired that he slumped to the ground. He sat there in a crumpled heap, growing colder and colder. His hands and feet felt numb. The whirling white snow swirled up and around him and covered his boots and snowshoes.

Now, the snow was covering him like a blanket. Perhaps, it was his friend, after all. He was starting to feel a bit warm ... and ... sleepy....

CHAPTER
FIFTEEN

Ryan thought he felt a hand on his shoulder. He must be dreaming. Then he gasped. In the midst of the white blizzard, a deeply tanned face came clearly into view. "Hello, son."

"Tówi?" Ryan could hardly believe it. He struggled to his feet and wrapped both arms around the big man's waist. "What are you doing here?"

"I heard shouting," said Tówi. "Wherever are you going in this storm?"

Ryan remembered his mission then and the whole tale came pouring out. Tówi stood beside the boy, sheltering him from the wind.

"Well, you are brave," said Tówi. "And you're mighty close to finding your own way. The trail is just beyond that clump of trees."

"But where are we once we get on the Original Road?"

"Only half a mile from the Davises' farm. You're almost there!"

Ryan was shaking with relief, but was ready to go.

"You look mighty cold," Tówi said.

"Not really," said Ryan, but he kept his hand in Tówi's big fur mitt as they walked along together. He was feeling awfully stiff.

"Are you all right?" asked Tówi. "I could carry you.... But it's not far.... Can you make it?" The wind kept sweeping his voice away.

Ryan plodded along as quickly as he could. "Of course, I can make it." But he still held onto Tówi's mitt.

"Land's sakes, what have we here?" Mrs. Davis exclaimed. She was standing at the front door, with wisps of grey hair falling out from under her mob cap. She was a short, plump, jolly woman with rosy cheeks and a kind smile that welcomed Ryan. She reached an arm around the boy and said, "Well, come in, you two, before you freeze us all to death!"

Ryan stumbled into the cabin and Tówi strode in behind.

"Bring me quilts, Donald!" Mrs. Davis shouted to her husband. "We have a frozen boy on our hands!"

"I'm all right, Mrs. Davis," said Ryan, trying to unwind his red, wool scarf. It was all frozen together and wouldn't budge. "It's Ann that ... She's ... "

"In labour?" said Mrs. Davis. "I thought as much. And she must be in a bad way to send you out in this weather. All right, Donald, let's get ready to travel. Ann's in trouble and we've got to get there fast!"

Ryan started shivering, not from the cold. What if, after all this, Ann … He couldn't finish his thought.

Mrs. Davis stopped her bustling about and turned to the boy, looking strong and kind at the same time. "Now," said Mrs. Davis gently, "tell us, Ryan. What's wrong?"

"Ann's having a lot of pain. That's not good, is it?" Ryan rushed on without giving Mrs. Davis any time to answer. "And Father isn't even there — only Alex and Kate and Geordie — and he nearly drowned and he's sick, too. So I pretended I was going to bed, and I snuck out to get you, but the storm was so bad, that I couldn't find your place. I couldn't … I … " Ryan broke off with a shudder.

Mrs. Davis and Tówi exchanged looks.

"He was very close to your place, Mrs. Davis. He could well have got here on his own," the man said calmly.

"And all's well that ends well," replied Mrs. Davis. She turned to her husband. "I'll get my things ready. You'd best hitch up the team, Donald." Then to Ryan, she said, "Get your outer things off and sit down over by that fire, now. And pour yourself and Tówi a cup of tea. You've a ways to go yet today, so you might as well warm up while you can."

Outside, the horses were moving restlessly in the cold air. They did not like the idea of heading out into the storm. Tówi helped Mrs. Davis up into the seat beside her husband. Then he swung up and sat next to her on the other side. Ryan jumped onto the back of the sled, dug himself into the pile of straw and flung a buffalo robe around his shoulders.

Mr. Davis gave the horses' reins a little flip and they started off down the lane. Tówi turned and looked at Ryan sitting just behind them. "You hungry?" he asked.

"I sure am," said Ryan. He'd hardly eaten all day.

"Here," said Tówi, holding out his mittened hand, "try some of Mrs. Davis's good bannock."

Ryan bit into the fluffy white biscuit, then poked Mr. Davis in the middle of his back.

"Can't we go faster?" he asked.

Mr. Davis turned around and stared down into the frightened eyes of the boy. "Well, we could, but then the horses might get worn right out and have to stop for a rest." He inched over in his seat. "Look through here, Ryan. You can see that snow — it's up to their bellies. They could even flounder and go down, and we might never get them up."

"Well, we could go a *little* faster!" said Ryan. "Or maybe we should go by snowshoe!"

"That might be faster … for you or Tówi. But not for Mrs. Davis. She's no youngster anymore and she's not used to wallowing through snowbanks. And she's the one who can help Ann — not us menfolk."

"Watch out, old man," said Mrs. Davis. "If I'm old, what does that make you?"

Mr. Davis and Tówi laughed.

Ryan was furious. Ann's life was in danger, Kate was

probably worried out of her mind, and these grown-ups were joking about it all. He pushed over the back of the seat and wedged himself between Mr. and Mrs. Davis. "Let me at that team," he shouted.

"Hold on there, son!" Mr. Davis said. "I know you're worried, but you've done all you can. Now it's time for us older folks to take over."

"But you don't understand!" said Ryan. "Ann's dying! We've got to get there!"

Mr. and Mrs. Davis exchanged looks, then strong hands clamped down on Ryan's shoulders. It was Tówi. He pushed the boy back into the straw.

"Ryan," he said, "we cannot go any faster. Mr. Davis knows his team and they're going as fast as they can. You have to understand that. Here I thought you were so brave making it to the Davises' all by yourself, but now you're not being brave or even sensible. You know horses, Ryan. You must not push them harder than they can stand."

Mrs. Davis turned around and leaned over, touching Ryan on the shoulder. "This is Ann's first baby, Ryan. She'll be in labour for hours before the baby comes. Pain is normal with childbirth, and she's not in any danger yet. I'll be there in lots of time."

"But my mother died!" Ryan cried.

"She was having twins. Ann isn't. Calm down. We'll make it in time."

Ryan sighed as the sled climbed slowly up and down the snowbanks. The sled runners left an uneven trail, which disappeared into the trees behind them.

Then he noticed that the path was being blotted out. More snow! That was all they needed! Mr. Davises' old team would never make it!

CHAPTER
SIXTEEN

Ryan jolted forward under the buffalo robe as the sleigh came to a full stop. He had been dozing, he guessed, but now that he was awake, his worries flooded back. Up on the front seat, Mr. Davis and Tówi were whispering to each other.

He crawled over the straw and poked Mr. Davis in the back. "What's the trouble now?"

"We're giving the horses a rest," said Mr. Davis.

Tówi gave Ryan a sympathetic glance and then looked back to Mr. Davis. "You know it's not far through those trees to the O'Carrs' cabin. If Mrs. Davis could use her snowshoes and let me guide her, I think we could get through a lot faster than the horses can go round. Suppose I ... "

"Yes," said Ryan, turning back. "Mrs. Davis, please,... "

Mrs. Davis looked down at the boy. Under his toque and scarf, his forehead was creased with anxiety. "Yes, Ryan, I can do that," she said kindly.

Ryan grabbed Mrs. Davis's snowshoes and started to strap one onto her boot. In just a minute, they were both on.

"Thank you, Ryan," said Mrs. Davis. "Now you can help me down out of this sled." Ryan helped Mrs. Davis make her way to the back end of the sled, where Tówi was standing ready to hand her down. "Now, my bag," she said. Ryan scrambled up to the front seat and grabbed her things.

Tówi and Mrs. Davis started off, and Ryan threw his own snowshoes onto the nearest snowbank and stood on them before fastening them to his boots. Then he started off as quickly as he could.

"Hey," shouted Mr. Davis. "Where in thunder do you think you're going?" Ryan didn't answer. He was too busy catching up with Tówi and Mrs. Davis.

After a fifteen-minute hike through the bush, the three travellers strode out into the snow-covered meadow and looked at the O'Carr cabin. A steady line of smoke was spiralling out of the chimney.

Ryan made himself go even faster. He must find out what was happening! Gasping, he reached the front stoop first and struggled to take off his snowshoes, which were already freezing to his boots. He flung them off quickly, rushed against the door, and threw it open. He stumbled inside in a gust of wind and snow.

Kate was lifting a big pot of boiling water from the hearth. She set it down and hurried over to the door.

"Oh, Ryan!" she cried, throwing her arms around her brother and choking back tears. "Thank God. You're safe."

"Is she …?" said Ryan. A loud scream tore through the open doorway that led to the downstairs bedroom.

Ann was alive, but in what condition? Ryan bit his lip so he wouldn't cry.

"Did you bring Mrs. Davis?" Kate asked.

"I'm right here," said Mrs. Davis, sailing through the doorway. "And I've birthed more babies than I can count. Do you have lots of boiled water, Kate?"

"Yes," Kate answered, with relief.

"Good!" said Mrs. Davis. She peeled off her coat and scarves, then held her hands over the fire to warm them.

"Hurry!" said Ryan.

"I must wash first," said Mrs. Davis, looking hard at Ryan. "And I want you out of here."

"But how is Ann?" Ryan stood his ground. "I have to know!"

Ann screamed again, and Kate rushed to the bedroom. When she came out, she spoke to Mrs. Davis in a voice too quiet for Ryan to hear what she was saying.

Ryan remembered Tówi and stepped outside. Tówi was still standing a short distance from the stoop. "How is she?" he asked.

"I don't know," said Ryan. As he stood in the open doorway, Kate picked something off the table and went over to the front door.

"Hello, Tówi," said Kate, looking over Ryan's head.

"He found me and took me to the Davises'," said Ryan.

"He was almost there anyway," said Tówi, smiling. "How is Ann?"

Kate was still frowning, but didn't look as frightened as before. "Mrs. Davis says she'll be fine. Now, Ryan, here's a basket of johnny cake and some fresh milk.

You go to the shanty with Alex and Geordie. They have a little fire going over there." Then she turned to Tówi. "You have some, too. Thank you again. Mrs. Davis would never have made it without you."

"… and Ryan," said Tówi, looking down at the boy beside him.

"Yes, Ryan … in that storm … "

"You have a brave young brother."

Kate smiled through her worry. "Well, there's Mr. Davis," said Kate. "I have to leave you now." The door closed and she was gone.

Tówi smiled and took the food Ryan offered him. "You go on to the shanty. Mr. Davis and I will tend to the horses."

Ryan raced as quickly as he could in the deep snow to the gently swaying cabin, still fastened to the trees at the corners. It would be good to see Alex. He could even stand to see Geordie, too, come to think of it.

A little stream of smoke rose from the chimney. Ryan opened the door and peered inside.

"Ryan! You're back!" Alex shouted. Geordie jumped down from a bag of wheat, raced over to the returning hero, and gave him a big hug.

"Hmmmpurr," said Bobcat, smelling Ryan's basket. He jumped down from his grainbag perch.

"Food!" said Geordie, as he grabbed two yellow cakes from the basket.

"Are you all right?" Alex asked. "We were awful worried."

"I'm fine," said Ryan, smiling. Then he sat down on a sack of cornmeal and told Alex and Geordie all about

his adventures. Geordie listened intently, his mouth full
of food and his eyes wide open. But Alex's response was
even more satisfying. He clapped Ryan on the back.

"Well, Ryan, I'm impressed. I don't think I could have
done what you did. You're the bravest fellow I know!"

◇

Bang! Bang!

"Open up!" It was Father.

Alex reached the door first, threw back the bolt, and
opened it. Father stood there in his heavy raccoon coat. He
look tired, but was smiling. Ryan knew that all was well.

"Any news yet?" asked Alex.

"Sure is," said Father. "You boys have a baby sister —
a wee baby sister!"

Then Father stepped over and clasped both arms
around Ryan. He was silent for a few minutes. "Ryan," he
said at last, "I know you saved the baby's life. If Mrs.
Davis had not come in time to help, the baby might have
died, and Ann ... well, I just couldn't take that again —
not after your mother ... " Tears glistened in his eyes.

"Is Ann all right now?" asked Alex.

"Yes, Ann's fine, but she needs a great deal of rest.
Mrs. Davis is going to stay and help Kate for a few days
— to give Ann a chance to recover." Then Father turned
back to Ryan. "You were very brave, Ryan. To head out
in a storm like that. Now, not letting Kate or Ann know,
that was ... but it has turned out for the best. It was
very brave, my boy, very brave." Father pulled out a big

red handkerchief and blew his nose.

Ryan smiled up at his father.

"And Kate told me how you saved Geordie, too. After such a morning and in that ice and all … " Father seemed to be choking up. He had the handkerchief out still and kept wiping his eyes with it. "I could have lost you, Ryan," he said, sitting on a grain sack near his son.

"I prayed a lot," said Ryan, squirming. It felt strange, being praised so much by Father. "Now there's one thing I want to do," he said, changing the subject.

"What's that?"

"I want to see my sister!"

"You've earned that right and then some. So come now. In fact, you can all see the baby," said Father, "if you're very, very quiet. Ann's asleep."

The three boys pulled on their coats and boots and charged through the door. A slight breeze blew snow off the branches of a maple tree next to the cabin and dropped it on top of them. Ryan brushed the snow off his toque. Father and the three raccoon-fur figures plodded along in single file toward the big cabin. The storm was over and at last the sky was brightening.

At the door of the cabin, Father lifted the latch and opened the door. Kate and Mrs. Davis were sitting quietly by the fireplace. "Take off those boots and coats," Kate whispered. She was bossing them again, thought Ryan. But Kate was smiling.

"They want to see the baby," whispered Father.

"Don't make a sound," said Kate.

The three boys tiptoed across the floor in their sock

feet. Ryan led the way, Alex followed close behind, and Geordie walked a few paces behind the two of them. Father held the door open.

Just inside the bedroom, a little brown cradle stood beside the big bed. Father's finger was pressed to his lips. None of them made a sound as they stepped up to the cradle.

There was the baby wrapped in woollen quilts. Only her tiny red face and head were uncovered. Her eyes were tightly closed. But then there was her hair. It was not like a baby's. There was a lot of it — thick, curly brown.

"She has Ann's hair," said Father.

Just then, Ann opened her eyes. She smiled and held out a hand to Ryan. "My hero," she said. Her fingers reached out. "Alex told me … you went for help."

Ryan took Ann's hand and smiled. Then Alex bumped up against his back.

"I was awful worried," Alex said. "Now I know what you went through last summer, Ryan. But I sort of knew you'd get through all right. I told Ann that, and she believed me."

"Yes, twins are extra special that way," said Ann. "And my little girl will have two wonderful big brothers!"

Ryan and Alex smiled at each other, and then they smiled at Ann.

"We'd better go, now," said Father. "Ann needs to sleep."

The man and the three boys stepped back into the warm, bright kitchen.

"Well, boys," said Father. "Now you have two sisters."

The twins glanced at Kate. The new sister might be

special, but she would never replace their first sister. Kate smiled at them. She knew what they were thinking, and she understood.

"I wish she'd been a boy," Alex declared.

"I'm glad she's a little girl," said Ryan. "And she's going to be real pretty — just like Ann."

Alex gave Ryan a look, and opened his mouth to speak. Then he closed it again. Finally, he said, "Ryan, let's go outside and have a snowball fight."

"Yes, let's," said Ryan. His blue eyes were sparkling at the thought. "We could build a fort. Kate, couldn't you come out, too?"

"Sorry. I have to get supper," said Kate.

"Don't bother," said Mrs. Davis. "I brought plenty of victuals — beef stew and fresh bread and butter. You go right ahead, Kate."

"It'll be you and me against the twins," said Geordie. "Let's go, Kate!"

Kate smiled. "All right, boys. Here we come." She hurried over to help Geordie into his coat.

Alex and Ryan were out the door long before Kate and Geordie.

"This might be our last snowball fight with Kate, you know," said Ryan. "One of these days, she'll be too grown-up."

"Well, let's make it a good one, then," Alex said.

The boys grinned at each other. Times had changed, but they would make the best of it.

PART FOUR

The Twins' Treasure

CHAPTER
SEVENTEEN

Maple blossoms were hanging down from the trees like jewels as Ann stepped out the front door, carrying the baby in her arms. Ryan sometimes thought she looked like a queen, the way she walked, so elegant. But the baby wasn't acting like a queen. She was yelling and squawking, just like a little piglet.

Alex came stumbling out the door, half-awake, pulling on his breeches as he walked.

"About time you woke up! Father and Ann are just about to leave!"

"No, it's about time Father left for King's Town. Another couple of days and the furs would have been all mouldy!"

"Oh, come on, Alex. You don't know what you're talking about!" Ryan was amazed at how Alex could argue all the time, even when he was half asleep.

The new baby, Mary Ann, had short, flat feet. And even worse, her soles turned in against each other. Ann had waited impatiently while winter turned into a wet spring. Now the roads were dry enough for travel, and

Father was taking her and the baby to King's Town, to consult with Ann's father, the army doctor. Ann was all set to go on to New York, if necessary — her father knew a surgeon there. And she was happy to be on her way at last. But Father was worried. There wasn't money for a surgeon's fee, let alone a trip to New York. The only coin the O'Carrs were likely to see this year was whatever Father managed to get from the furs.

"Well, we're off!" Father barked from the wagon. "Keep up that cultivating while we're away. I need to start seeding when we get back. It'll be a couple of weeks, but the time'll pass faster than you think, so no loafing on the job!"

"'Bye now, my brave boys," said Ann, handing Father the baby and jumping up on the seat beside him. "We'll be back before you know it!"

"Yup, my little men," said Father. "You hold the fort. I'm depending on you! And *no swimming*!" He raised one eyebrow and stared hard at Alex.

Alex hated being called Father's little man and being ordered around like an unpaid hired man. Ryan didn't like being Father's little man either, but he never said much because he liked the farm. Only sometimes he'd sneak off and read one of Ann's books when he was supposed to be working. Then he'd get a good scolding from Father.

The boys watched the wagon as it disappeared among the maples and poplars.

"I'll bet Father will be back in a week," said Ryan. "He'll just sell those pelts, pick up the supplies, drop Ann at her parents, and come back lickety-split."

"You know, I'll bet you're right," said Alex.

"And he'll expect everything to be ready for seeding as soon as he hits the ground!" Ryan laughed. "He'll never change!"

"One good thing, though," said Alex, beaming, "if he leaves Ann and the baby behind, it'll be just like old times!"

"Well, not quite," said Ryan. "Kate won't be here. And I'll sort of miss Mary Ann."

"I won't! I never asked to have a baby around, and now she's going to cost us plenty!"

"Alex, what a mean thing to say!"

"Okay, okay. I take it back. Come on, let's get to work."

The twins sauntered toward the barn, where Baron, their trusty guard-dog, bounded out of the lilac bushes and barked at the bright morning.

"Oh, Baron, don't be so happy. We have a horrible day ahead of us," Alex grumped. Then he stopped in his tracks. "Oh, Ryan ... "

"What?"

"Remember all that baking Ann left for us? There'll be way too much if Father gets back in a week. Maybe we should start eating now!"

Ryan looked at Alex and grinned.

In seconds, they were back at the house, pulling pies and cakes out of the larder.

"Wow, apple crumble!" said Ryan, helping himself to a large serving.

"Hey, go easy! There's johnny cake and oatmeal cookies and a hundred different kinds of pies ... "

Knock, knock.

Someone was rapping hard at the front door.

The boys stared at each other in startled silence. It couldn't be Father. He'd walk right in. Alex raced over to the door and flung it open. "James!" he squealed.

Ryan brushed the crumbs off his shirt and looked up to see a shaggy black beard with a man behind it. He looked exactly like a villain in a pirate book. And his beady eyes were just a bit too close together. But there was Alex treating him like a long-lost brother.

"James, meet my twin, Ryan," Alex said, dragging his old friend over to the table by one hand.

James chuckled. "Well, you do look like two peas in a pod!"

"Yeah … guess you didn't notice when you dropped me off in the cornfield last summer!"

"Nope … can't say as I did. I high-tailed it out of here as fast as I could."

"Too bad! You could've stayed for my funeral!"

"Your … your what?"

"Well, everybody thought I'd drowned, so … "

"You don't say. There they were singing you into the ground, and you walk in all tanned and fit as a fiddle!"

"You mean sunburned and bitten up by bugs! I was a mess."

"Sure," James laughed, his eyes twinkling under his bushy eyebrows, "but you were very much alive!"

"Come on and have some pie, James," Alex urged. "There's raspberry and strawberry and apple crumble if Ryan hasn't eaten it all."

"What's this? A celebration?" James said, stroking his beard.

"Well, we don't usually have this much good stuff, but the folks left this morning for King's Town. They'll be gone for a week or two. So our stepmother left us all this baking. It doesn't matter when we eat it."

"Oh, now I see," said James, grinning hard. "While the cat's away, the mice will play. I remember you doing that one hot day last August. And I bet you have work to do today, too."

"Yes, we do," said Ryan shortly. He wished that Alex hadn't told James that their parents wouldn't be home for a long time. It would be safer for him to think they'd be home soon. A whole gang of pirates could be lurking in the woods waiting to take over their place.

"Well, I have an offer for you," said James. "Ivan came with me. Remember him? He's waiting outside. The two of us could help you do some of that work."

"Ivan!" said Alex. He didn't like Ivan, the red-haired one who growled a lot and looked mean. "Why did you bring Ivan along?" he asked.

"Oh, it's good to travel with someone. Helps to cover your back."

"Oh," said Alex. "So you're going back for the gold ... with Ivan! I thought you were going back with me!"

Knock. Crash. Knock.

Ryan dropped his spoon on the floor. This time it sounded as if the door was about to be demolished.

"Sounds like Ivan!" said James, smiling.

Alex went over to the door and pulled it open.

There stood Ivan, scowling and shifting his eyes back and forth across the room. "'Bout time you opened up the gates, you little scoundrel! I coulda bin waitin' out there in the bushes for days with you managing things!"

Ryan was fumbling around under the table, trying to pick up his spoon. But his hands were shaking so hard, that he kept dropping it again. As he straightened up and peered over the edge of the table, two green eyes with yellow flecks were staring straight at him.

"What!" Ivan bellowed. "There's two of them!"

"Sure, Ivan," said Alex, speaking more quietly than usual. "We're identical twins."

"Idiotic twinges?" said Ivan, guffawing and slapping his thigh. "Gawd help us. One of yous is already too many for this little caper!"

Ryan glared at Alex, but Alex was glaring at Ivan. *Great!* thought Ryan. *My brilliant brother strikes again! What do you do when your parents leave you in charge? You invite a bunch of cutthroats in for breakfast.*

"Help yourself to some good home baking," said Alex, inviting the red-haired thug to sit down at the table.

Ivan stomped across the floor in his heavy boots, leaned over the table, and scooped up a large piece of strawberry pie. He stood there eating it right out of his hand.

"So … are you going back for the gold?" Alex grinned.

"Yup, that's what we had in mind," said James merrily — as if he were planning a picnic, thought Ryan.

"Don't go sharing no secrets with that kid," said Ivan, his mouth full of strawberry pie. "He knows too much already."

Just then, Bobcat came barrelling in through the front window and headed straight for Ivan.

"What the …? Get that thing out of here!" Bobcat had jumped onto the pirate's shoulder and was hanging on hard. Ivan turned all red and started stomping around in circles.

"Get off me, you wildcat. I can't stand cats! You monster you!! Just get … get … " But there was no scaring Bobcat. Ivan flailed around and dropped his pie right on the toe of his boot, but Bobcat still hung on to his shoulder and was sniffing at the pirate's tousled red hair.

"Here, Mr. Ivan," said Ryan. "Just hold still for a minute!" The boy strode over and pried Bobcat away from his perch. "Don't worry. He just gets a mind to do that sometimes."

"Just gets a mind to, does he? Well, I have a mind to get out of here and leave you young twerps behind!" He stared at the boys and then at James.

"Leave us behind?" said Alex, his blue eyes shining like two beacons. "You were planning to take us somewhere?"

"Well, yes," said James. "We want you to join our treasure hunt."

"Do I get one-third?"

"No!" Ivan spluttered, scraping the strawberry pie off his boot and slapping it on the table in front of Ryan. "No kid gets a third of our gold!"

"*Your* gold!" Alex yelled. "It's not your gold. You stole it. Remember?"

"That's enough, Alex," said James, sounding like Father.

"I had a deal of trouble persuading Ivan you'd be of use to us as a decoy. You supply the victuals and help find the gold. Ivan and I will dig it up and we'll let you fill your pockets. That would be enough to buy you a farm in these parts."

"But I don't want a farm! I'm going to be a hunter!"

"Doesn't matter, you can use the money for something else then."

"Like Mary Ann's operation," said Ryan.

"Who's Mary Ann?"

"Oh, skip it," said Alex. "… but I sure could use the money! So, what's this about a decoy?"

"Well, son, me and Ivan here were down to Montreal this past while, and we've heard there's fellows from Quebec and King's Town that think they know where the gold is buried!"

"And you want to get there first, right? But why do you need a decoy?"

"Well, if anyone else sees me and Ivan heading for that bay, they'll suspect us right away. If you come along, you'll give us an innocent look. Especially since you're small for your age."

"Small!" shouted Alex. Now he was upset. "I just haven't started to jump up yet. Father was short at my age, too."

Ryan thought he saw a sparkle in James's eye, but he wasn't sure.

"I can believe that," said the man, "but right now you look about ten."

"Ten!" shouted Alex. "I'm *twelve!*"

James grabbed a blue-checkered handkerchief from

his back pocket and blew his nose. Ryan wasn't sure, but it looked as if he was laughing!

Meanwhile, Ivan was leaning against the wall, doubled over. "Good going, James!" he spluttered between guffaws. "You just dropped a pebble in a hornet's nest."

"Sorry!" said James when he'd cleared his throat. "I forgot little fellows were touchy." Ivan guffawed again, but James's grin quickly turned remorseful. "I know how brave you are, Alex," he hurried to say. "That's why we asked you to share our adventure."

Alex stopped frowning and said, "I'll go if Ryan will come, too." The men turned their eyes on Alex's twin.

Ryan stared right back. Suddenly, he was in a position of some importance. So he decided to make the most of it. "I'll go — on one condition."

"What's that?" asked James.

"You'll have to help us cultivate. Then, we'll have to find someone to look after the livestock. We can't just run off and let the animals starve."

"Yes," said Alex. "I was forgetting."

James stared at Alex. "Yes, you were. So why don't we leave Ryan to take care of things, and you can come alone."

Alex looked from one pirate to the other, and decided. "I want Ryan, too. It won't be any trouble for our friend Tówi to feed the livestock. Father often helps him out. Tówi won't mind."

"Maybe he won't let you go," said James.

"Oh, we'll tell him that you're lost and we have to show you the way and we're not sure how long we'll be gone. He'll feed the animals till we get home."

"Is it settled then?" asked James. "Are you both coming?"

"As soon as the work is done," said Ryan.

Ivan groaned slightly as he scooped out another piece of pie — blueberry this time. It was dripping down both sides of his hand.

Ryan, watching, discovered he was not hungry anymore.

◇

Five days passed, and the farm underwent a complete change.

Ryan and Alex coaxed the makeshift cultivator — a triangular-shaped tool made of pieces of timber filled with pegs — across the fields with the help of their skinny old horse, Bess.

James worked up the soil by shovelfuls, and Ivan worked hard too. Once Ivan got in the field, he worked almost as hard as a regular plough horse. The strange team of boys and pirates finished the cultivation in record time, and even managed to plant all the hay seed — more work than Ryan and Alex could have finished in three weeks.

Now they were packing the last supplies for their great gold hunt. Ryan was sitting on a bench at the edge of the dooryard, stuffing food into his backpack: dried meat, fresh rolls, johnny cakes, and cornmeal for more johnny cakes, which they would make along the way. He'd stopped for a minute to sample one of the rolls, but unfortunately, James had emerged from the house and told him to get moving.

Alex was sitting on the other side of the dooryard cramming containers of bear grease into his backpack. He also packed extra moccasins and shirts. He would never forget running through the woods in bleeding bare feet, covered by mosquitoes and black flies. The bear grease would keep the bugs away, and the moccasins and shirts would make life on the road much more comfortable.

Ryan tied his pack tight and leaned it against the bench. "I'm going in to put our note on the kitchen table. Then I'm ready to go!"

"A note on the kitchen table. Well, I'll be ... " said Ivan. "I never leave notes anywhere! I just leave whenever I please!"

"Sure, Ivan," said James, "you don't leave notes because you never learned how to write!"

Inside, Ryan was struggling with the last part of the note. The first part, explaining how the pirates had arrived at the door, had been easy. But how could he explain why they'd gone away? In the end, he just said that Alex's pirate friends needed guides. They'd decided to go because the men had helped them finish the farm work. Father should be happy about the farm part, but Ryan hated to think what he'd say when he returned to an empty house. Luckily, he and Alex would be miles away by that time.

Ryan set a pickle jug on top of the note so it wouldn't blow away, checked the fireplace to make sure the fire was really out, and walked over to the door. He wasn't happy about leaving the place and he felt guilty as he was lifting the latch. But once he stepped outside, he said to himself, "In for a penny; in for a pound," and strode over to where Alex and the pirates were waiting.

"Which way are you planning to go?" asked Alex.

"Straight south and then across the lake to the peninsula," said James, wiping his forehead with his blue-checkered handkerchief. The sun had barely risen, but the day was already hot.

"How will we get across the lake?" asked Alex. "You didn't bring any boats that I can see!"

"Exactly," Ivan growled. "You can't see it. We hid the canoe right in your maple woods. The trees keep secrets!"

Ryan and Alex gave each other a quick glance. Did the woods keep any other secrets? Was the whole crew of pirates going to jump out and capture them? Ryan thought not. They would have done that long before now if that was the plan. And James and Ivan wouldn't have stayed to do the seeding. Ryan smiled at James. Ivan might be a monster, but James seemed to be all right.

The men and their decoy-boys picked up their packs and walked out of the yard, just as Tówi was walking in to do the first round of chores.

"Goodbye, Tówi, we'll be back as soon as we can!" said Alex, saluting like a soldier.

"Just make sure you do get back!" said Tówi, looking as if he did not believe their outrageous story. He shook his head and laughed. Then he turned and walked over to the barn, with Baron running happy dog-circles around him.

Ryan looked back longingly at his home, then turned abruptly and marched on. The line of boys and men snaked its way into the woods and disappeared in the underbrush.

CHAPTER
EIGHTEEN

"This sure beats work!" said Alex, as Ivan and James dug the canoe out from under moss and reeds in the O'Carrs' woods near Hay Bay. The slim boat was made of strips of birch and cedar bound together with pine resin and rawhide. It wasn't big, but the pirates said it was strong enough to withstand even a bad storm. Ryan wasn't so sure, though, as he watched the two men hoist the canoe over their heads to carry it along the trail. Out in Lake Ontario, the craft would bob around like a toy.

"Now, you go ahead, Alex," said James kindly. "Your brother can bring up the rear. Both of you keep your eyes wide open."

They fell into line along the trail through the woods. Robins and warblers were singing their morning songs, and the smell of pines filled the air.

"What if we bump into our neighbours?" Alex shouted back to James.

"Tell them your cousins came to visit," said James, "and you're helping them find their way back home."

"They know we don't have cousins in these parts."

"Well, tell them we're old friends of your father's or mother's. It doesn't matter. Ain't you got any imagination, boy?"

"I guess," said Alex.

"And if you don't know the folks, then say you're travelling with your Pa and his brother."

"But you don't look like brothers," said Ryan, looking at James's shaggy beard and Ivan's thick red hair.

"Well, we ain't twins!" Ivan laughed loudly at his own joke. Then his whole face suddenly flamed red and he turned sideways under the canoe, toward James. "Why in blue blazes you bothered with these two is beyond me. We don't need no decoys. We need speed and we won't get it with these dimwits. Get them outta here!"

Alex ran down the trail to Ivan and landed a flying punch on his arm. In seconds, Ivan set down the front of the canoe, turned, and swatted Alex with the back of his hand. Alex went crashing to the ground.

Dropping his end of the canoe to the ground, James jumped between Ivan and Alex. "Watch it, you two!" shouted James, pulling Alex to his feet.

"He called us dimwits!" yelled Alex.

"That kid's a loose cannon," said Ivan. "He'd better learn to control that temper, or else—"

"Or else what, Mister?" said Ryan, stepping up beside James. "You're the one with the rotten temper!" He was shouting at Ivan but he was so scared that his hands were limp by his side.

"This is no way to get places," said James. "Now,

march. All of you, march in line."

The unwieldy line took form again and wound its way closer to the bay.

In about ten minutes, they had emerged from the woods and were standing in line from the shore of the bay. The water was calm, and the men slid the canoe easily into the water.

"Maybe we should go back," Ryan mumbled into his brother's ear.

"No way!" grumbled Alex. "You know how badly we need that money."

"I guess," said Ryan, "but who says they'll give us any? They'll probably dump us and run when they don't need us anymore."

"James will keep his promise!" Alex was heading down to the shore now to the very spot where he'd gone swimming the summer before.

"I'm not so sure!" Ryan said, grabbing his brother's hand. "Ivan wasn't along when you travelled with him before."

"But James is in control," Alex answered. "Not Ivan."

Maybe, thought Ryan, but about one thing he was sure. Ivan could not be trusted. James — well, he didn't know.

When they came out of Hay Bay and into Lake Ontario, white-capped waves were rolling in toward the shore. "Let's wait," said James. He flopped down onto the beach. Alex dropped onto the ground beside him; then Ryan followed. Ivan paced back and forth, scanning the lake and chewing his lower lip.

"You aren't looking for another British ship, are you, Ivan?" Alex asked. He'd never forget how they'd been chased the summer before. He thought he was brave enough, but he never wanted to go through that again!

"Of course, I am, you addlebrain!" Ivan growled. "We're not going on a picnic, you know!"

"We're not worried much about the British," said James. "We're more worried about the fellows who helped us bury the loot. They're more apt to be a problem. Some of them may have beat us to it!"

"Well, if that's the case, then no one will chase us," said Ryan. He was starting to wish the money was long gone so he and Alex could stay out of trouble. Then he thought about little Mary Ann. She needed that doctor. "Still, it would be nice if we could get there first."

James's mouth widened into a smile and his eyes twinkled as he reached over and gave Ryan a slap on the back. "Glad to have you aboard, Ryan."

Ivan stopped chewing his lip and pointed at the lake. "Look!" he said. "Those waves are finally calming down. Let's push out."

Together, the four flipped the canoe and slid it into the cold, dark blue water.

◇

"Any ships coming?" Alex yelled back at Ryan. They'd reached the other side of the divide and were heading out farther in Lake Ontario, around the southern shore-line of the peninsula.

"No," said Ryan, who was sitting at the back of the canoe looking east. "No one is following us, Alex.

And that's the third time you've asked in the last few paddle strokes. Are you expecting someone?"

"No. He's just remembering the last time we were here," said James. Alex cleared his throat and gave James a cold stare. He didn't want his brother knowing how scared he'd been.

Ryan took no notice. His eyes were glued to the horizon and he was loving the sound of water clapping against the canoe. "Nothing a bit like a ship ... as far as I can see. Of course, there could be a canoe somewhere!"

"Right, Ryan. You just had to say that, didn't you!" said Alex. He was clutching the sides of his bench seat and swinging his feet back and forth, trying not to feel scared.

"I think it's your turn to keep watch," said Ryan. "C'mon down here and I'll give you the spyglass." Ryan stood up to make room for his brother as Alex inched forward.

"Sit, down, you confounded nincompoops!" Ivan growled. "You'll capsize us and we'll all drown before we even see that gold!" Ivan's green eyes shone with anger and greed. And the yellow flecks turned brighter.

A wave slapped against the side of the canoe and Ryan plunked back down on the crossbar at the stern.

"Ryan's doing fine, Alex!" James shouted. "Stay where you are!" Alex sat back down weakly. Just like the last time he had come this way. He wasn't feeling so good.

Then Ryan saw something. At first, he couldn't tell what it was and so he didn't say a thing. Then slowly, the small speck turned into a long shape as it moved along the shore. It was a canoe like their own. It nosed into the lake and then headed back toward the shore. *Probably, a farmer taking time out for fishing,* he thought. He sure wasn't going to tell Alex it was there. His brother looked scared enough already.

◇

"Are we almost there yet?" Alex yelled over at James.

"Not long now, and we'll turn into the inlet," said the pirate, dipping his paddle slowly and steadily into the water.

"But we've already been *out* here for hours! In the bateau, it only took us a short time!"

"Right, you little twerp!" Ivan hissed. "That's because there were a bunch of hefty men rowing — and only one dumb little boy not pulling his weight!"

"I'll paddle for you!" Alex said, trying to pretend he wasn't seasick.

"Oh, no, you won't! You'll have us at the bottom of the lake in no time. When I canoe, I do the paddling — not little pipsqueaks that don't know a blade from a bow!"

The waves kept chopping against the bow, and Ivan kept slicing his paddle into the water. Alex had to admire him for his strength. When he got behind a plough or a paddle, things happened pretty fast. Too bad he had such a nasty temper. He might have been almost likeable if he weren't always going around like a smoking volcano, waiting to erupt.

"What'll you do if a bunch of other pirates show up on the beach at the same time as us?" Ryan asked James.

"We'll share the loot with 'em!" Ivan butted in. "We're buddies — all of us!"

James gave Ivan a poisonous look.

I guess James isn't buddies with all the pirates, Ryan thought. *And that's probably a good sign.* Ryan was dying to know how James got stuck hanging around someone like Ivan. But he didn't dare ask. He looked over at the shore through his spyglass instead. The other canoe had left the shoreline and seemed to be approaching them at top speed.

Ryan turned around to say something, but before he opened his mouth again, he caught a fast glimpse of Alex. His brave brother was still clutching the seat beneath him, and his face was greenish white.

Better not say anything to Alex, thought Ryan. *He's either seasick or scared silly or both.*

Ryan spoke to James instead: "Are we going as fast as we can?"

"That we are, my boy! That we are! Why do you ask?"

"Ummm … How soon will we turn into the inlet?" Ryan was trying to catch James's eye without attracting Alex's attention. But that was impossible. Alex's eyes were glued on Ryan.

James realized Ryan's problem. He nodded his head and pointed back down the lake to indicate that he, too, had seen the approaching canoe.

Smart for a pirate, thought Ryan. *And a decent fellow, too.* Without moving a muscle, Ryan said, "I wish we could go faster. I'm sick of being on the water. I'll *never* be a sailor."

James nodded again. "We can turn into the inlet now," said James. "Let's plough into those waves, Ivan."

The two men cut their paddles into the water with tempest-like speed, and both boys felt the canoe shoot ahead.

"What's the rush?" Alex shouted.

Nobody answered, and the only sound to be heard was James and Ivan breathing heavily as they kept up their vigorous pace.

"Hey, I've been through this before," Alex yelled. "Someone's chasing us, aren't they, Ryan!"

"No ... no one's coming after us. It's probably only a small canoe like ours. And it's a long way behind. Probably a farmer taking time off to go fishing."

"Taking time off?" Alex said, wrinkling his nose and shaking his blond hair off his forehead. "A farmer? Taking time off in the middle of spring seeding time? No farmers do that."

"Right," said Ryan. "Except us, of course!"

"Well, we're different! We're looking for gold!"

"Well, maybe *he* is too! James! Ivan! Paddle faster! I think some of your buddies are trying to beat us to the beach!"

"So be it," said James. "We're paddling as fast as we can."

"Yeah, let them get there first," said Ivan. "They can do the diggin' and we'll share the loot. We have ways of makin' people cooperate!"

Ryan rolled his eyes to the heavens. He did not want to hear exactly how Ivan made people cooperate.

Right now, he wished he was in the barn, shovelling manure. That would be much safer than shovelling sand with Ivan the Terrible.

"UUUGGGMMmmpphpFF!" James yelled as the canoe ground to a halt.

"What are you *stopping* for?" Alex yelled back.

"Hit a sandbar, you flippin' dunderhead!" said Ivan. "Cantcha keep yer eyes open?"

"Well ... " Alex did not want to tell anyone that he'd been looking far out of the canoe so he wouldn't get even more seasick.

Ivan wasn't listening anyway. He and James had jumped out of the canoe and were pulling it over the sandbar. Only a few more paddle strokes and they'd be on shore ... and the gold digging would begin!

CHAPTER
NINETEEN

"C'mon, you lazy thumb-twiddler! Dig faster!"

Alex was feeling better now that he was on solid ground, but he was still a bit woozy and couldn't possibly shovel as quickly as Ivan and the others. It was also rather scary being on this beach — right beside the burned-out hull of the bateau. The remaining ribs and boards looked like a giant's bones. Uneasily, Alex wondered if his bones would be the next ones on the beach. With Ivan around …

"Hey! Look out!" Ryan was shouting and pointing out to the middle of the lake.

"Yeah!" said Alex. "There's that canoe again. She's coming in to our beach!"

"Quick," said James. "Pull our canoe over this last hole and let's sit down on it and start eating. Pretend we're on a fishing expedition and having a picnic."

"But we don't have any fishing poles!"

"Right. Well, then we're just exploring. I'm your uncle and Ivan's my friend, and we're taking you out to teach you how to canoe and survive in the woods."

"Well, that's the closest to the truth we've got yet," said Ryan. "But it's still not true."

"Well, tell the truth and you'll lose all that gold," Ivan barked. "Never pays to tell the truth!"

Ryan looked to the heavens and contemplated a cloud scudding across the springtime sky. *What am I doing here,* he thought, *stuck on a beach with a lying pirate, trying to dig up stolen gold?*

"Hein! Salut les gars!"

"What gibberish is that?" Ivan asked, scowling.

Three sunburned strangers had pulled up on shore, greeting them in French.

"What are you boys after?" Ivan boomed.

"They don't understand English!" said Ryan.

"It may be a trick," James mumbled. "They may under-stand English very well. Don't say a word you don't want them to hear. Understand?"

The twins nodded.

The smiling fishermen looked a lot like James. They had dark hair, brown eyes, and bushy eyebrows. But their beards were neater and they looked as if they were just having fun. One of them was waving a huge pickerel in the air. The second stranger headed for the woods and came back with kindling for a fire. Another prepared a spot for a fire while the first man started cleaning his fish.

"Wow!" said Alex. "I'm gonna make friends with them." He grabbed a handful of johnny cakes and strode over to the French fishermen.

"Careful!" said James. But Alex paid no attention.

Alex was disappointed when the fish cleaner refused his offer of the fresh, yellow cakes. But the next one smiled at Alex and took three.

"Ah! C'est bien! Merci, mon petit!" he said.

Mon petit? thought Alex. *Doesn't that mean 'little guy'?* He wasn't sure he liked that label. He wanted to hunt and fish like these men, and he didn't like them calling him small.

"I think you've made friends," said James as Alex came back and sat down on the canoe.

As he sat crossed-legged on the soft sand, Ryan was trying to size up the men. They were talking now, and he wished that he understood what they were saying. Their voices rose and fell in a kind of rhythm. Were they planning an ambush? Did they know the gold was here?

Half an hour later, the most delicious smell came from the French fishermen's fire. The pirates and the boys did not have to think twice when they were invited to join them. They ate their fill and drank the beer and spring water that the men had brought with them. Everyone spoke in his own language and no one seemed to understand anyone. But they all enjoyed the meal — except when one of the fishermen pulled a log out from under Ivan just as he was about to sit on it. The sturdy pirate crashed down on the sand in a heap.

Ivan was on his feet in an instant looking furious, but James stepped up fast and clapped him on the back, laughing. "He meant no harm. Look!" The cook was handing out another plateful of delicious-smelling fish.

Ivan glared at him suspiciously as he took the dish of food. But his eyes lighted up as he ate.

◇

"Hoo-hu-woo!"

Alex woke up with a start. Was that Ryan giving him the owl call?

"Hoo-hu-woo! Hoo-hu-woo!"

It had to be Ryan. Alex scrambled out from under James's canvas canopy, where Ivan was snoring loudly and Ryan was … Ryan was also under the canopy, fast asleep.

Well, thought Alex, *that must be a real owl, then.* He gazed at the pine and maple forest and listened hard again. But all he could hear was the shuffling of feet against the sand! Okay, now who would *that* be? He wasn't sure he wanted to know.

Moving ever so slowly and quietly, Alex peered around the edge of the canvas canopy and saw the French fishermen sliding their canoe out into the water.

So they were going to leave without saying goodbye. Well, who cared? He didn't. Alex watched the men with his eyes half-closed. Then, as the moon went under a cloud, he saw two of them step soundlessly toward James's canoe. He froze on the spot. They were drawing closer.

Alex rushed over to where James was sleeping and pounced on him. "They're after our canoe!" he whispered hoarsely.

James woke up in a split second. "Wha ... What was that?"

"Those men are taking our canoe!"

James poked the snoring Ivan. "Quick, man, we gotta get our canoe!"

"Shner ... ferip ... schnooork!" Ivan sounded like a cross between a pig and a firecracker as he dragged himself out of dreamland. But once he was awake, he was up and running.

"Oh, no, you don't, you lousy — !" Ivan bellowed as he barged into one of the fishermen in a running tackle.

He punched the man on the nose and sent him sprawling out on the sand, then turned like a bull to the second one. He grabbed that one by the collar, threw him down on the ground, and sat on him.

Alex had to admire his skill. For once, Ivan was putting his temper to good use.

Meanwhile, Fisherman Number Three had high-tailed it out of Ivan's range and was dragging the first victim down the beach toward their canoe.

"Okay, Ivan," said James, "you can stop sitting on the poor guy now. Let him go. He's not going to bother you anymore."

Ivan stood up slowly and his second victim groaned and started crawling away down the beach. He joined the other two in their canoe and the three paddled away faster than Alex had ever seen anyone paddle. In minutes, they were out of sight.

"Alex, you saved our canoe!" James smiled. "We owe you one!" But he wasn't looking at Alex. He was looking at

Ivan as if to say, "See? Young boys can be a big help in a pinch!"

"Alex just cried wolf. I did all the biting," Ivan grumbled.

"That's true, but if Alex hadn't sounded the alarm, we would have … Good Lord, we would have had a long walk home!"

Ryan crawled out from under the canvas and yawned. "What's all the noise about?" he said.

"Oh, nothing," said James. "Go back to sleep." Ryan said nothing and crawled back into the tent.

Alex stared at James, offended. James had called his great brave adventure "nothing." He crawled back under the canvas beside his brother.

"Ryan, you'll never guess what just happened!" No answer. Ryan was fast asleep.

◇

KER-CHHUUUNNNK!

James's shovel had whacked something hard that sounded hollow. An echo came from the other side of the bay in the pre-dawn darkness.

Pay dirt!

A big whoop rose from Ivan, who was digging away on another part of the beach. He came pounding over and gazed into the hole as if he was praying to the heavens. "Well, boys, we found 'er. And to think no one got here before us!"

"Yes, our timing was good. Not right away, but not too late either!" James agreed.

Everyone dug in, throwing clumps of wet sand on the beach. The sound of it took Alex right back to that day last summer when the pirates dug the gold into the beach — the soft sand, the water filling the hole, the explosion as the captain blew up the bateau.

What a nightmare! But they'd survived and now … here was their reward. Or was it? The thought kept coming back. This gold hadn't just fallen from the sky. It belonged to someone — and James and the pirates had stolen it!

"UUMMMmmppph!" said Ivan as he stretched out beside the hole and reached down to pull up the cask. Lake water swirled around a corner of the container, but it was stuck fast. Even Ivan couldn't make it budge.

"Hey, Ryan," said Alex. "Why don't I lean over and grab the cask and you hang onto my legs and pull as hard as you can!"

They did that, but the cask didn't move.

James and Ivan dug deeper, and Alex and Ryan kept pulling. Still nothing.

"If we can just move it enough to let the water underneath, we'll break the suction," said James.

So they kept on. The lake's waves were splashing right over Alex but he didn't let go and … THOOOP! The cask gave a sudden lurch.

They knew they had broken the suction but still had a lot of digging and pulling before them. After another fifteen minutes, they finally got it loose. Ivan threw his spade in the air and danced a jig around the beach. James just quietly opened the container and reached in.

Coins, coins, hundreds and hundreds of coins. Alex and Ryan sat and watched as the two pirates fingered the money lovingly in their hands. Ryan could not believe that so much money could look so … common.

"Hey, it doesn't even glow!" Ryan said to Alex. "I thought it would be really shiny!"

"Me too!" said Alex. "But I don't care! Now we'll have enough to send Mary Ann to New York!"

He grinned at Ryan, and Ryan smiled back. They were both happy they'd come — in spite of everything.

The first birds of the morning were beginning to send twittering sounds from the woods and the light was growing stronger.

"Well, looks like daylight," said Ivan. "Guess we'd better close up this cask and get out of here before those fishermen come back!"

"I doubt they'll be back," James said. "They were glad enough to get out of here, and they didn't say a single suspicious word the whole time!" He laughed at the others' looks of amazement. "I didn't let on I understood French for the same reason I told you fellows to keep quiet in English. And they didn't hide anything from me. So I know they didn't have a clue the gold was here."

Very smart, for a pirate, thought Ryan, for the second time.

James was going on. "Yes, they were just regular fishermen, looking for pickerel and salmon. Apparently there's famously good fishing around here. Fishermen come up the river from Montreal and travel to King's Town. But they hardly ever come this far."

"They're probably back at King's Town by now," said Ivan. "I think we scared them plenty. I probably broke that fellow's nose — I heard it crack. Boy, did it bleed!" He seemed to enjoy the memory.

Alex and Ryan gave each other a worried look. What would Ivan do if he got angry at *them*?

"Well, let's head back, James," said Ivan. "We'd better drop these kids off and be on our way."

"Don't forget! We get our share!" said Alex, forgetting to be afraid.

"Yeah, yeah," said Ivan, chewing his lower lip and shifting his green eyes right and left.

Alex glanced over at James, but he was looking down. "Let's pack up," he said. "You boys get busy with that tent."

James and the boys took the canvas tent down, but Ivan sat beside the treasure, wrapped his legs around the cask, and stared at the gold.

Alex couldn't forget Ivan's shifty look. While Ryan and James were busy folding the tent, he walked over to Ivan and stood just a few feet away, watching. Ivan was passing the gold coins through his fingers, back and forth, back and forth, oblivious to anything around him. Alex leaned over so his face was only a few inches from the gold, and dug his hands into it right beside Ivan's. He let the gold jingle through his fingers, too.

Startled, Ivan lifted his head. His eyes glittered ferociously. Then he raised his right hand, made a fist, and punched Alex right on the nose. Alex fell backwards onto the sand.

"Owwwww!" screamed Alex. "Owwwww!" He held

his hand over his nose as the bright red blood ran between his fingers and into the sand around him. His screams echoed right around the bay and into the forest.

James and Ryan dropped their half-filled packs and came running to Alex. Ivan just stuck the top back on the cask of gold and dragged it to the canoe.

"Alex, Alex, what happened?" said Ryan.

"He hit me," Alex yelled. His nose was still bleeding and it hurt so badly that it seemed to be stinging right up to his eyes, now streaming with tears.

"Here," said James. He drew out his blue-checkered handkerchief. "Pinch your nose shut with this, real tight now." Then he turned to Ryan. "Take a rag from our pack and wet it in the cold water and hold it over Alex's nose — higher up, at the bridge." Ryan hurried to the water's edge.

"Now, Alex, quiet down or it won't stop bleeding. It'll take only a little while to clot — if you'll shut up. It's not broken." He took Alex's hand and put it to the handkerchief. "Now, hold this tightly, right there."

James stood up then and walked over to Ivan, who was throwing things in the canoe as if nothing was wrong.

"Now, we'll thee thomthing," said Alex. His nose was so plugged his words were all blurred. "Jameth will beat him up."

"He deserves it," said Ryan, his face all red with anger. "If he doesn't, I will."

James reached over and touched Ivan on the shoulder. The bully turned sharply, and the pirates faced each other.

The boys waited for the big smashing sound of Ivan's nose being flattened, but … James just mumbled something to his fellow pirate that the boys couldn't even hear. Then he turned away and started packing again.

Ryan was furious. "You beast," he yelled, doubling his fists and running toward Ivan. But James intercepted and pushed Ryan onto the sand — right on his seat.

"Whose side are you on?" Ryan yelled.

"The fighting is over," said James. "We'll have no more of that! We have work to do, and we won't get it done by fighting."

"But he hit my brother!"

"Well, your brother should not have been digging into the gold. If he'd kept packing as he was supposed to, this would not have happened. You two had better mind your own business and do as you're told from now on."

Alex winced as he held the handkerchief to his nose. Had he been wrong in trusting James? Maybe he was more like Ivan than he seemed. Alex wished he'd never got on that pirates' bateau last summer. It was *his* fault that he and his brother were in this mess. If he could cry, he would, but that would hurt his nose too much.

Finally, Alex's nose stopped bleeding, but he looked terribly pale. Ryan felt a little sick now, too, but he put his arm around Alex, and together they headed for the canoe. Alex sat on the floor and laid his aching head on the middle gunwhale.

"I feel real sick," he mumbled. And he felt even sicker when he remembered Ann and Father. What if they came home early and found him gone again — with no gold to show for his efforts?

"You just rest," said Ryan. "I can manage the spyglass."

About fifteen minutes later, their canoe shot out of the inlet and into the white-topped waves of Lake Ontario.

Ryan sat with the spyglass glued to his right eye. "All's clear," he shouted above the noise of the waves. "There's not a vessel in sight — anywhere."

"Keep watch!" said James. "Don't let your guard down for one minute." He returned to paddling.

The violent motion combined with his previous nose-bleed made Alex feel sicker than ever, and Ryan was having trouble keeping his balance as he scanned the horizon all around.

"We've got to travel closer to shore, where the water's calmer," James called to Ivan.

"We won't make good time that way," Ivan growled back.

"We can't risk upsetting in these waves," said James. "Not with the gold. We'd never find it in the lake."

Ivan grimaced and shook his red hair, but he did not argue.

CHAPTER
TWENTY

"Alex," Ryan whispered, "I've been thinking that gold isn't ours to keep."

"I've been thinking the same thing," said Alex. He didn't like to agree with Ryan, but he knew his brother was right. Those coins had been stolen from someone, somewhere.

It was three days later and the boys and the pirates were back at the southern tip of Hay Bay. In another day, they'd be home. The trip back took longer as they'd travelled more slowly and kept close to the shore.

The cask of gold lay inside the canvas tent between the sleeping pirates, but Alex and Ryan had been turfed out. It was James who'd told them to bed down there.

"I still think James is my friend," said Alex.

"Then why did he make us sleep outside? There's lots of room under the canvas."

"Maybe he's hoping we'll escape," said Alex. "Maybe James wants us to escape so we're safe from Ivan. I don't trust that thug."

"It's the gold, you dimwit!" said Ryan. "He's afraid

we'll steal the gold."

"Dimwit! You're starting to sound like Ivan!"

"Thanks for the insult! But the gold is the problem, Alex. That's stolen gold. We must not keep it!"

"They're the ones who stole it, not us!"

"It's still stolen, and you know the commandment: 'Thou shalt not steal,'" insisted Ryan stubbornly.

"And you know that if Ivan gets it all, he'll use it for bad things. We need it for good things: for the farm, and for Mary Ann. She may never be able to walk right if her feet don't straighten out."

"I know that," Ryan sighed and looked away from Alex.

"If we take it for Mary Ann, how is that wrong?"

"I can't explain, Alex, but I know it is," Ryan said. He sounded sad, but Alex could tell he was determined. "We have to get the gold to Father. He can return it to the land office or the fort in King's Town. That much gold doesn't disappear without someone knowing where it belongs."

Alex was silent for a while, then he sighed. "I guess you're right, Ryan, but it sure is hard. We need that money so badly. Now, tell me — how on earth do we get it away from those two?"

"I don't know," said Ryan. "For a start, we could see if they're asleep."

"Maybe," said Alex, "but we'll have to be awful quiet."

They crept around to the trees at the back of the tent, where the pirates' heads were likely to be resting. "The woods are so thick," whispered Alex. "There could be a bear. Did I tell you about that bear and her cubs — the ones in the raspberry patch?"

"Oh, just about a hundred times. Now, stop talking!"

The twins peeked under the canvas and saw James sleeping peacefully. He didn't look like a pirate when he was asleep. He looked like somebody's father.

Then they looked over at Ivan.

"What!?" Alex whispered.

"Quiet!"

Ivan was shaking the pine needles off his clothes and tucking his shirt into his pants. Next, he put on his big walking boots.

No problem with that, thought Ryan. *If it was morning, that is. But in the middle of the night?*

As the boys watched, their worst fears came true. Ivan headed straight for the cask of gold, picked it up like a baby, and hugged it as he sneaked out the front.

"Hey!" Alex whispered…. "No! Hey! HEY YOU!" This time he was shouting.

Then he dived under the canvas and landed right on James.

"James! James! Ivan woke up! He took our gold!"

James was up in a minute, tucking his shirt in as he ran out in his bare feet.

But Ivan was nowhere in sight.

KER-CRASH-PLUNK!!!

"Ohhhh, someone just got hurt bad," James said.

Alex looked at James, and James looked back at Alex.

"Ivan?" said James.

"Ryan!" said Alex.

The two of them raced to the back of the tent, and

there was Ivan, sprawled out on the ground. The cask of gold had rolled down the side of a big rock and had come to rest at the foot of a huge oak.

Moonlight was shining down on Ivan's boots, which weren't laced up properly. And it was also lighting up Ryan's face, as he grinned away, holding the huge branch he'd used to trip the red-haired pirate.

At the sight of James, Ivan struggled up and threw a punch in his direction, but James sidestepped and Ivan fell forward. He didn't fall to the ground though. Instead, he just grabbed the nearest tree branch and hung on to it.

"What's the matter, Ivan?" growled James.

"I musta sprained my ankle when I fell. It's not workin' so good."

"Right! Poor you! You can't run away with all the gold!"

"Well, I heard these steps comin' toward the tent ... and I thinks, 'They're after the gold,' so I ... "

"Oh, no you didn't. I know you too well. You were going to take it all for yourself. You low-down thief!"

"We're all thieves if we take that gold," said Ryan quietly. The other three looked soberly at the boy.

"No one's a thief for taking pirates' gold," said James.

"But you're the pirates," said Alex. "You stole it yourselves, didn't you?"

A strange silence developed. Only the scampering sounds of small animals in the nearby woods and the washing of water against the shore could be heard.

"I think we should give it back, James," said Alex.

"I think we should."

"Oh, sure!" said Ivan. "You aren't going to listen to a couple of kids, are you?"

The silence got heavier.

"I don't know," said James. "I do need that gold. It's my ticket to a new and better life. I'll be using it for a good cause."

"We all want to use it for a good cause. But it's not ours to use," said Ryan. "So that makes it wrong."

James stared at Ryan.

"You're a bunch of hypocrites," said Ivan. "You want the gold for good causes, do you? Well, at least, I'm not a hypocrite. I want it for me! And I don't care who else needs it!"

The boys and James stared at Ivan. They all seemed to make up their minds at the same time.

"That settles it," said James.

"Yes," said Ryan. "We return the money. It's not ours!"

"I'll help you," said James, "if you don't rat on me and Ivan."

"We won't," said Alex with a sigh. "I guess I've always known we'd have to return it."

The tattered troop travelled another day by canoe, then a piece overland before they reached the O'Carr farm on the other side of Hay Bay. Even with the gnarled cane that James had carved for Ivan, it was slow going. But at least, that sprained ankle meant they didn't have to worry about Ivan running off with the gold anymore. He wasn't running anywhere.

"I don't suppose they'll be having another funeral," said Alex wistfully as the pirates and the boys entered the moonlit dooryard in the late evening of the second day.

"Don't be daft, Alex!" Ryan grumbled.

"Meeoooww ... yeooww!"

Bobcat dropped out of the big maple tree.

"Not that tomfool cat again!" Ivan shouted. "Get him off me!"

Bobcat protested and hissed, but after a bit of coaxing, Ryan and Alex managed to get his claws out of the pirate's shirt.

"Well," Father boomed as he strode out of the cabin. "I see the happy wanderers are home!"

"Father!" The two boys exchanged looks.

"You're home ... early," ventured Alex.

"Right you are, and surprised, too, I'll wager. We'll talk about your little escapade after your guests are gone. Though you did at least one good thing — you left a note this time."

"Yes," said Ryan. "We didn't want you to worry."

Father laughed so hard that the twins thought he was going to explode. The twins couldn't understand it.

Finally, Father wiped his eyes and held out his hand. "You're James, aren't you? I recognize you from Alex's tales about last summer. And you are—?"

"Ivan," the surly pirate growled. His attempt at a friendly smile was not too successful, and Father eyed him suspiciously.

James pulled a cask out from under the bundle of canvas at his feet, and Father looked his way again.

"What's … ?"

"It's gold," shouted Alex. "We brought back the pirates' gold."

"It was stolen from a British ship," James said carefully. "We've brought it back, but we don't want to return it ourselves. We might get hanged for stealing."

"Well, I've been wanting to thank you for saving my son last summer," Father said. "And now I know how to do it. I won't turn you in, and you can stay with us till your friend is better. Looks like he has a bad ankle."

"Thanks," said James. "But it's just sprained. And we'll be moving on in the morning. Ivan and I have other business to attend to. Though we'd be mighty obliged if you'd pack us some extra victuals for our trip."

Father went into the cabin to get some food, and Ryan and Alex showed the two men to the shanty, where they were to spend the rest of the night. Ivan went right in, but James hesitated at the door.

"Well, boys, in case you sleep in tomorrow, I'll say goodbye now. You were right about giving up the gold."

Alex looked up sadly at James. "I never thought you were a bad guy, James. But I did think … "

"I know. You thought I should have beaten up Ivan. Well, I warned him not to touch you again. And he didn't."

"Thank you, James. Now, don't worry. You can trust my father. He said he wouldn't turn you in, and he won't. He's tough sometimes, but he always keeps his word. You can count on that."

"Something like his son, eh? … a man of his word."

Alex grinned. "I'm going to miss you, James," he said.

"I'll be back," James promised, "sooner or later, God willing and the Devil not withstanding." He smiled beneath his black beard, and stuck out his hand. Alex shook it firmly.

Then Alex threw his arm over Ryan's shoulders and the two blond-haired, sunburned boys walked briskly up to the house.

In the morning, James and Ivan were gone.

EPILOGUE

"James! Is that you?" Alex yelled, tumbling out of the doorway. It was June, two years after the boys had returned with the gold, and Alex had spotted a sleek black stallion trotting into the yard. He couldn't quite see the rider against the rays of the setting sun — but it looked like James.

Ryan walked into the dooryard right behind Alex. As Father had predicted, the two of them had shot up like beanstalks. They were now fourteen.

The rider swung down from his horse, pulled a blue-checkered handkerchief out of his back pocket, and wiped his forehead. "Phew! It's just as hot on that road as it was when we ..."

"James! It *is* you! What are you doing here!?" Alex exclaimed.

Ryan just stood beside his brother and grinned.

James smiled at the twins. They could see the smile better now, because his beard was neat and trimmed. They had liked that old pirate beard, but somehow felt this one was better.

A two-year-old girl in a long yellow dress had run up behind Ryan and peeked around at the man and his horse. Her huge brown eyes sparkled with curiosity.

"And who's this little one?" James asked.

"Oh, that's Mary Ann — remember? Our baby sister. The one we …"

"The one you wanted to steal the gold for?" James laughed. "But she looks fine."

With that, Mary Ann was off running around the dooryard, trying to get Bobcat to chase a piece of string. Of course, Bobcat had no interest in such silliness, but Mary Ann didn't care. She could run and that was all that mattered.

"She's better because we sent her to a doctor in New York City — five times!" Alex explained. "When we returned the gold, we were given a reward, and that money paid for her treatments. And she wears special shoes with iron braces. You can't see them because her dress hides them."

"Ever since Mary Ann was a baby, Ann had to turn her feet several times a day," said Ryan, "but not so much anymore."

"At the rate she's going," said James, "I'll bet she could outrun the two of you."

"Oh, yeah?" said Alex. "She's not that fast yet. But then I had practice running with a pirate!"

"Well, I'm not a pirate anymore!" said James. "I'm a farmer now, and my place is not far from here."

In a few minutes, James had filled them in on everything that had happened to him since they had parted two years ago. He was soon to marry the daughter of a Loyalist farmer for whom he had been working.

"I guess he'll set you up with tools and young cattle," said Ryan knowledgeably.

James smiled at his earnestness. "Well, he's busy with his sons but, yes, there'll be a small dowry."

"The reward money we've been keeping for you will come in handy," said a deep voice behind them. It was Father, who'd come out to join the others. Ann was just behind him, followed by Kate. She'd come over for a visit from their farm just two miles to the east. It was clear that she would be having a baby soon.

"Where's this farm?" asked Father.

"Well, it's going to be farther inland, in Earnesttown, but we'll clear it with the help of Catharine's family."

"Where's Ivan now?" asked Ryan.

"Oh, he's working on the docks in Montreal. He'd like to farm, but he wasn't lucky enough to find work with a good family like I did. I'll share the reward money with him. That could help him buy his own place."

"Come in for fresh johnny cakes," said Ann.

"Thank you. I have fond memories of your baking, Ann," said James, winking at the boys.

"Hey, Ryan," Alex whispered, as the twins followed the others into the house. "Do you think we can persuade James to go north with us to look for that cave full of silver we've heard about?"

"You mean Meyers' Silver Cave?"

"Yes, that's the one."

"Don't forget there are lots of bears up there. Besides,

nobody really knows where the cave is."

"Yeah! That'll make it an even better adventure! I'm going to ask James to come along."

"I hope you don't," said Ryan, throwing an arm around his brother's shoulder. "But I know you'll try!"

HISTORICAL NOTE

The O'Carrs and the Shaws came to what is now Canada because they were loyal to Great Britain during the American Revolutionary War (1775–1783). The British lost the war, and the many colonies that had fought against the British formed a new country called the United States of America. People who were loyal to the British were unwelcome in this new country, so they moved north to what remained of British North America. They were called United Empire Loyalists.

The majority of the Loyalists were originally from Great Britain and Europe. Some of the Loyalists were Six Nations Iroquois people, and about 10 percent of the Loyalists were African-American former slaves, who had fought for the British during the war and earned freedom. About 80 to 90 percent of the first settlers were former military men and their families.

The first waves of Loyalist settlers went to what are now the Maritime provinces, and later groups settled in the Eastern Townships of Quebec. The O'Carrs and others who travelled to Quebec were encouraged to go even farther west — to the north shores of the St. Lawrence River and Lake Ontario and to the Bay of Quinte area (near today's Belleville), which was then considered part of Quebec or "Canada." By 1791 Canada's population had grown so much that a governor, John Graves Simcoe, was appointed for the new administrative district of Upper Canada (today's Ontario) as distinct from Lower Canada (today's Quebec).

The Loyalists were among the earliest immigrants to what is now Ontario. Before they arrived, the area had been inhabited mostly by Aboriginal peoples. The Loyalists were helped for a while by the British government, but like all immigrants, they had to work hard in their new land. During 1787, they contended with a severe lack of supplies, summer drought, and an extremely harsh winter. Many perished in what became known as the Hungry Year. Those newcomers who survived did so due to the generosity of Aboriginal people and of more established settlers.

Immigrant children were as hardworking as their parents, and mature beyond their years in many ways. Like Kate, Alex, and Ryan, they were also strong, brave and resourceful. However, since there were no schools, and parents did not often take the time to teach them how to read and write, many children were illiterate.

Although the central family in this story is fictitious, I have borrowed their names from real people. My great-great-great-grandfather, Daniel Carr, of Irish ancestry himself, was a volunteer in the Loyal Rangers during the

American Revolutionary War, and received five hundred acres of land in Earnesttown, which bordered on the east side of Fredericksburgh. Later, his son moved inland to Rawdon Township. My Grandma Carr was the granddaughter of Sarah Ann Bleecker, the granddaughter of Mary Meyers, who was the main character in my novel, *Meyers' Creek*. Sarah Ann married Daniel Stapley, whose parents came directly from England: they were Richard Stapley, a surgeon in the British army, and his wife, the former Lady Anne Banks. As you can see, I have moved some of these characters into this story.

Like the O'Carr family, Ontario's first pioneers and their children, toughened by their war experience and farming background, kept their rugged independence and loyalty to family, Great Britain, and God, along with a deep sense of duty and a capacity for hard work. With determination and great courage, they kept struggling until life improved in their new country.